TURNING TOWARD THE SUN

If I Never Speak of It
No One Will Know

CEIL WARREN

Library of Congress Cataloging-in-Publication data is available.
ISBN paperback: 13-978-1-7341279-1-1
ISBN ebook: 13-978-1-7341279-0-4
BISAC categories:
Fiction/Small Town & Rural
Fiction/Romance/Later in Life
Fiction/Friendship

Westchester County, New York
Printed in USA

This is a work of fiction. All of the characters, names, places and incidents portrayed in this novel are products of either the author's imagination or are used fictitiously. Any resemblance to actual persons, living or dead, events or locales is entirely coincidental.

Turning Toward the Sun. Copyright 2019 by Ceil Warren
Cover design by Asya Blue
Edited by Mark Mathes
Bottom cover photograph by Ceil Warren

Ceil Warren
Visit my website at www.ceilwarren.com

To the memory of my mother, Madeline.
Thanks, Mom, for teaching me how to dream.

Reviews

"Wuthering Heights meets The Andy Griffith Show. — In her debut turn, author Ceil Warren paints a cast of characters with a backstory like Heathcliff's and heart like Aunt Bee's. Set on a single day in the New Englandish village of Stones End, the story centers on Arthur, the reliable but passionless bachelor who owns the town printshop and harbors a deep secret. As each kooky resident of the village is introduced, flashbacks illuminate the characters and the strong relationships that make this day inevitable. Warren has a flair for dialogue. The characters' playful and compassionate back and forth swaddle the reader in a cloak of friendship. Until you see how it turns out for your friends, Arthur and the rest, you won't be able to put the book down."

—L. Moneypenny, Westchester County, NY

"This poignant, delightful book will be savored and remembered! Ceil Warren weaves a suspenseful web of long-ago love in a small bucolic village in rural Connecticut. A mysterious letter turns a routine day upside down packed with intriguing twists and surprises. Quirky characters, including a philosophical bench, offer deep insight into life's challenges and meaning."

— Jacqueline Kutner, President,
Bronx County Historical Society, Riverdale, NY

"I got so close to Arthur and his family of friends I could almost hear them breathe. I laughed, cried, and chuckled at the endless kindnesses, grace, and vulnerabilities of the characters who left a hole in my heart. Can't wait for the next book in the series."

—Dr. Wally D. Borgen, New London, NH

"Feel-good book of the year! A rare pleasure when an author takes the reader into the soul of a character. I cherished this richly woven, witty, soul-searching journey as Arthur struggles to shake off his past and take a path toward an unknown future."

—M. Cardinale, Dutchess County, NY

"Loved it! I was completely captivated by this wonderful novel celebrating life and all its messy complexities. Profound, witty, engaging story that constantly moves forward with fast-paced, hysterical dialogue, heart-stopping, heart-aching and stand-up-and-cheer moments. Turning Toward the Sun is filled with relatable characters: quirky, lovable, flawed. The story unfolds as 62-year old Arthur receives an unexpected letter which causes him to wrestle past demons, fight to keep a 40-year-old secret hidden and attempt to find an answer to a decades-old question. Will he find the redemption and answers he seeks?"

—N. Dmytrijuk, Orlando, FL

"I found Turning Toward the Sun a winning mix of intrigue and charm. Throw in an anthropomorphic bench named George, zany sass-talking friends, hilarious antics, life at its heart-wrenching best and love at its most tender moments and you have an utterly satisfying read."

—M. Piri, Bronx, NY

"Arthur is determined to keep his forty-year-old secret hidden. His nosy, well-intentioned friends are equally determined to find out what he's hiding. Who will emerge triumphant in this epic battle of wills? Don't miss this one-day journey with Arthur as he struggles to answer one of life's biggest questions."

—K. Whitton-Grzanka, South Carolina

"Allow yourself the great pleasure of reading Turning Toward the Sun. You'll give yourself the gift of a sunny day surrounded by fabulous friends. Truly heartwarming!"

—A. O'Connor, Westchester County, NY

"In her first novel, Ceil Warren delivers a compelling narrative of one man's struggle to replace bitter memories with hope for the future. I was captivated by the moving vignettes that serve as a reminder that we are all capable of compassion. In the end, I was first surprised and then serenely content with Arthur's resolution and its unexpected consequences. He had finally taken his father's advice which are words for us all to live by: 'Let go of the day's worries each night so there's room for tomorrow's joys.'"

—L. Carpenter, Westchester County, NY

"It was exciting to read this novel of Arthur and his dilemma of a long-lost love. The author carries the intrigue of a mysterious letter with panache. The story line flows beautifully drawing the reader into the action. You cannot wait to turn the next page. I was captured by the richly developed characters who drew me to their quest of helping Arthur. Eagerly awaiting your next feel-good story!"

— J. Weremeichik, Sarasota, FL

"Thoroughly enjoyable read. A delightful story with eccentric and charming characters, who are a pleasure to get to know. I hope I can make another trip to Stones End in the future."

—K. Faughnan, Dutchess County, NY

Acknowledgments

Thank you to my amazing sisters, Barbara, Margaret, Kathy and Natalia. Your encouragement and enthusiasm were greatly appreciated. It's what kept me moving forward. You're the best!

Heartfelt thanks to my wonderful friends, Jackie, Michele, Wally, Ann, Lorraine and Linda who cheered me on to the finish line. Will definitely return the favor if ever you write a book.

Can't leave this page without a big thank you to my editor, Mark Mathes. I'm grateful for your insightful editing, your patience, generous sharing of knowledge and for being a joy to work with.

And last, but definitely not least, many thanks to Asya Blue for her amazing cover design and formatting. You took the stress of out the process with your professionalism and awesome talent. You're one in a million!

Turning Toward The Sun

	Deep, Dark Secrets	1
Chapter 1	Start of a Crazy, Mixed-up Day	2
Chapter 2	Diversionary Tactics	4
Chapter 3	Mrs. Kruchinski, The Gossip	7
Chapter 4	A Charming Place to Live	9
Chapter 5	The Café	12
Chapter 6	Martin, The Quiet Observer	15
Chapter 7	The Nuclear Explosion	18
Chapter 8	Berris, Master of All Things Colorful	20
Chapter 9	Adapting to the Plan	22
Chapter 10	History for Dummies	24
Chapter 11	Routine in Tatters	26
Chapter 12	Call to Action	30
Chapter 13	Bittersweet Memories	33
	Unwelcome Changes	35
	A Labor of Love	40
	Darkness Falls	47
	A Powerful Emotion	50
	Forgiveness and Redemption	52
Chapter 14	Emergency Council Meeting	60
Chapter 15	Getting Closer	63
Chapter 16	The Great Coffee Feud	65
Chapter 17	Rounding Up the Troops	70
Chapter 18	The Decision	72
Chapter 19	The Incident	76
	Rounding Up the Troops – Continued	82
Chapter 20	Caroline, Internet Surfer Extraordinaire	83
	Rounding Up the Troops - Continued	84

Chapter 21   Walter, Resident Virtuoso 85
Chapter 22   Start of the Council Meeting. 90
Chapter 23   Father Gregory, The Spy 95
Chapter 24   Do We Know Arthur Covington
at All? 98
Chapter 25   Constance, William and Willie 104
Chapter 26   Constance and Willie 111
Chapter 27   Constance Moves Forward 114
Chapter 28   A Village Friendship. 117
Chapter 29   Opening Pandora's Box 120
The Picnic 124
Doubts Creep In. 131
Ana Felicia's Debut. 133
A Night of Anguish 137
Chapter 30   The Burning Question 139
Chapter 31   An Unexpected Visitor 142
Chapter 32   Opening the Letters 153
Chapter 33   Preparing for Ana Felicia's Visit 157
Chapter 34   Ana Felicia Remembers 159
Chapter 35   The Second Emergency Council
Meeting. 169
Chapter 36   Frantic Preparations 173
A Romantic Table 174
Constance Says Goodbye. 175
Arthur Gets Ready 177
Chapter 37   The Visit. 180
Chapter 38   The Long Wait. 188
Chapter 39   Ana Felicia's Story. 190
Chapter 40   The End of a Crazy Mixed-up Day 200
Chapter 41   One Final Task 210
Hello Fellow Reader 212
How to Use This Book in Your
Book Club Discussion Group 213
About the Author – Ceil Warren 214

TURNING TOWARD THE SUN

Deep, Dark Secrets

There is never an explanation of why some days are so very ordinary while others are extraordinary. Today, without giving it any thought or planning, was going to be extraordinary. Extraordinary for Arthur and everyone he knew.

For Arthur lived in the tiny village of Stones End where life moved slowly, gossip traveled fast and it was simply impossible to keep deep, dark secrets hidden forever. And Arthur harbored a deep, dark secret...for the past 40 years.

As each decade passed, Arthur was lulled further and further down the proverbial rabbit hole...*if I never speak of it, no one will know.* But this was Stones End, after all, so he never really stood a chance.

You see, as fate would have it, his friends were a lot better at uncovering deep, dark secrets than Arthur was good at keeping them hidden.

CHAPTER 1
Start of a Crazy, Mixed-up Day

There was a sense of unease clinging to the day as Arthur stepped onto his front porch with coffee in hand. He shuffled over to his bench and sat down with a thud spilling some of the precious brew. The sound of his creaking knees made him feel as old as the river he looked out upon.

He built the bench with his own hands and thought of it as a good friend, an old friend, one he could count on to offer a good sit down.

For the past 30 years or so, Arthur enjoyed long conversations with his bench and decided that such a good and old friend should have a name. He always liked the name George. It spoke of his ancestry, conjuring images of English royalty and Greek fishermen. And, so he named his bench George.

Like the tiny Connecticut village, the house where he lived was also called Stones End and there were simply no records if the village was named after the house or the house was named after the village.

It was a modest two-story home, barely 1,500 square feet, with living room, kitchen and dining room filling its first floor and three bedrooms upstairs. More than enough room to suit a bachelor's needs. He rarely hosted overnight guests. Make that never.

For 93 years, the old stone house fought off every violent storm the Northeast threw at it and lived to tell the tale as they say. Arthur loved the house with its wrap-around porch that gazed upon the ancient Housatonic River flowing just 200 feet beyond.

The slowness of village life suited Arthur. Although he had to admit, Stones End had a unique defense against the tedium of small-town living. For in this tiny village, the residents had a particularly quirky approach to life which kept the daily business of living lively.

They simply cared about everything and anything passionately. Residents still talk about the two-week argument between Karl, the landscaper, and Horace, the mail carrier. They argued about the quality of dirt.

Arthur greeted each day with the same ritual of opening his front door, inhaling morning air scented with wet dirt and river mists, making his way over to his beloved bench and taking that first satisfying sip of hot black coffee.

He allowed himself one cup per day on doctor's orders but Arthur loved coffee and would drink it all day long, if only he were allowed.

Arthur's life was a well-ordered and predictable one and he came to rely on the sameness of his daily routine. It gave him comfort like an old worn bathrobe you simply cannot part with.

But this day was different and Arthur knew it. Trouble was lurking like a far-off twister charging right at you. He didn't see it at the start of the day. But before day's end, his deep, dark secret would be a secret no more and life would change forever in the tiny village of Stones End.

CHAPTER 2
Diversionary Tactics

"I'm tired," Arthur said giving a good stretch. The words were unfamiliar to him at this time of day causing an uncomfortable feeling to pass through him. It was a feeling of waiting for the other shoe to drop and that was never good.

"Why are you tired? You got a good night's sleep," said George.

"I can't rightly say, George, I'm just tired. You know the kind of tired I'm talking about. You feel it right down to your bones."

George knew that feeling well just as he knew the unopened letter on the kitchen table was the cause of Arthur's edginess. It was more than worry. It was fear of the unfamiliar path beckoning him.

But George knew Arthur well and had every confidence he would figure it out...eventually.

"Today feels different somehow but for the life of me, I can't imagine why," Arthur said.

Arthur's mind whirled. *How could a letter cause such dread? What could possibly be said after 40 years? Why don't I just march into the kitchen and open it? Ridiculous idea, considering I can't even lay my eyes on it without cringing.*

In the end, he thought, *foolish old man.*

Arthur looked up to see that first light was in the eastern sky shuffling off the last stars. *I'd better get ready to open the shop.* But to his amazement, he did not move. *A strange day,* he thought. And the uneasiness passed over him again as though he was precariously hanging on to a cracking tree branch.

"It's that letter," George said.

"Please don't bring it up, George."

"Arthur, it's been sitting there for two weeks. Just open the bloody thing and get it over with. Aren't you curious?"

"There's a reason why I can't bring myself to drag it all up again," Arthur said in a shaky voice. "That chapter of my life is hidden away and that's where I want it to stay! Opening it up would simply...."

Arthur couldn't finish. His forehead wrinkled and his body shuddered as painful memories threatened to take over the quiet of his day. *Keep it hidden,* said a voice in his head.

Arthur knew George was right. *That blasted letter is weighing on me.*

"Now you're talking," said George.

"I'm not opening the letter," Arthur said through clenched teeth. "I just need a diversion. You know, something to take my mind off things."

"Forgive me, Arthur, but I don't think creating diversions is in your bag of tricks."

"Well, I'm sure I can think of something," Arthur fired back.

And Arthur set his mind to the task. The moments felt like hours.

It must be something different. Something I've never done before, he thought drumming his fingers on his knee. *I always lose myself in a new project.*

But as hard as he thought, his mind came up blank. "Oh, this is impossible," he said, slapping the arm of the bench. "Blast it all, George is right."

As Arthur sat poised to admit defeat, an idea started to form. It seemed crazy. *It is something I've never done before.* And then without any discussion or argument, Arthur announced to George: "I'm taking a day off!"

Now this concept was as foreign to him as landing on the moon. Arthur had not taken a day off in the 52 years he'd been working. George, as you can imagine, was shocked.

Wait till everyone hears this one, George thought. *It's going to be a hell of a day, that's for sure.*

CHAPTER 3
Mrs. Kruchinski, The Gossip

As Arthur and George sat trying to figure out what one does on a day off, footsteps stomped up the path. Arthur recognized them as Mrs. Kruchinski's heavy-footed walk. *This is trouble.*

Mrs. Kruchinski owned the village bakery where she made the best chocolate babka on Earth. But in Arthur's humble opinion, she could be a bossy woman always telling everyone what they were doing wrong and how to do it right.

Mrs. Kruchinski rounded the bend and caught sight of Arthur sitting on his bench. Her shock was so apparent, she jumped as if she'd just seen a ghost and lost her footing. The sight was so comical, Arthur nearly laughed out loud but valued his life too much to laugh at Mrs. Kruchinski...and certainly not to her face.

"Arthur, why aren't you getting ready for work?" she demanded.

"I'm tired," Arthur replied and heard George whisper, "You're lying."

"Tired! Who isn't tired? Are you sick?"

"No, I'm not sick. Just tired."

And in true Mrs. Kruchinski fashion of taking control, she announced, "I'm sending for the doctor!"

"Stop your foolishness, old woman, and be on your way," Arthur called out and then thought to add, "You'll be late opening the bakery."

This, he was certain, would get Mrs. Kruchinski moving for she was never late opening. She considered being late for anything tantamount to a mortal sin requiring a trip to the confessional.

Arthur held his breath waiting to see if his clever plan would work. Mrs. Kruchinski glanced at her watch then stood staring at Arthur.

"Uh-oh, George, she's not taking the bait."

"What's she doing?"

"Just standing there looking confused."

Finally, Mrs. Kruchinski uttered her well-known grunt of disgust, gave a dismissive wave and headed into the village, but not before saying, "We'll see about this. And never again call me Old Woman!"

"Phew, that was a close one."

"And we're off," said George.

"What's that supposed to mean?"

"Are you kidding, Arthur? You know as well as I, that Mrs. Kruchinski can't wait to spread the word that you're not going to work today. Then, tongues will start wagging which will lead to speculation. And speculation will lead to worry and...."

"OK, George, I get the picture. Just stop there."

George stopped. But knew he had his work cut out for him. Arthur had a head made of concrete at times.

CHAPTER 4
A Charming Place to Live

If villages could talk, Stones End would speak of old-world charm and graceful living. Stone, brick and clapboard shops and houses dotted the landscape. Mighty oaks and majestic elms wrapped their twisted outstretched branches around its perimeter for hundreds of years. Stone walls still snaked over open fields marking eighteenth-century property lines and pony express trails.

The mere two-block expanse of Main Street was a kaleidoscope of color. Awnings of brick red, goldenrod yellow, hunter green and burnt orange hung from every shop. White stone planters overflowing with cascading flowers and shrubs scented the air with hints of rose, peony and lilac.

Shopkeepers competed with one another with embroidered door banners. Loaves of bread marked the bakery, a candy-striped pole for the barbershop, a manuscript for the bookshop, googly-eyed fried eggs for The Café and more.

Arthur's senses came alive whenever he walked down Main Street. Fried onions escaping from The Café triggered a mouth-watering hunger. Opera music floating from the barbershop carried him to Carmen's Seville and Mimi's Paris. And whiffs of fresh-baked bread wafting out the bakery door put him right back in his mother's kitchen in Greece.

And a cherished aspect of Stones End was that every shopkeeper called out a greeting. This simple acknowledgment of his presence was comforting to an old bachelor living a solitary life.

Arthur didn't know which was his favorite shop in the village. He loved them all. But if he were pressed to choose one, he would have to say it was The Page Turner bookshop.

The inviting atmosphere of overstuffed armchairs, all with floral prints, dozens of rows of shelves crammed with books, magazines and periodicals, warm scatter rugs everywhere. It was his cup of tea.

Arthur indulged in a guilty pleasure each time he walked into the shop. Upon entering, he would stop, close his eyes and wait to see which aroma would capture his senses first. Would it be the smell of fresh-brewed coffee, the wonderful earthiness of the books, the tantalizing aroma of hot baked goods or the woodsy scent of a roaring fire?

The shop always gave the feeling of walking into the home of a dear friend and Constance Whitestead, the proprietor, made him feel like a treasured guest.

Stones End was a village where there may have been more benches than people. And Arthur had everything to do with it. They were in front of the shops, around the village square and even throughout the park.

He carved each of the benches with whimsical fairy-tale and mythical creatures: Puss in Boots, Cheshire Cats, and even a fire-breathing dragon. His handiwork delighted young and old and was worthy of estate gardens in France, Italy and England.

At the top of Main Street was the village square. It was the site of the annual flower and planting fest which left behind a riot of color from spring to autumn.

A two-tiered stone fountain gurgled an eternal spray of water high in the air. Ancestral trees with gnarled branches and prickly stuccoed bark watched generations of villagers chatting on benches, tourists throwing a wishful coin in the fountain and workers grabbing a quick lunch under their cooling shade.

Although the village was small, the residents referred to the two-block area of shops as Downtown and the square as Uptown.

Arthur walked each day in the park along the river path fast enough to count as a cardio workout. He lunched where the river narrowed and crashed over granite that survived eons of relentless pounding.

He imagined the park as an ancient, primitive world. Everything was alive: tall grass stretching to reach the sun, garden snakes wriggling smooth bellies along cool stones, hummingbirds heartily drinking from fluted flowers, digger bees constructing underground fortresses and flights of birds soaring hard toward the freedom of the sky.

The park was never-ending in its impossible complexities of movement, color and scent. It spoke an unheard language of life, death and rebirth through the ages. Serene and balanced yet wild and free. It nourished Arthur's soul and its mightiness humbled his heart.

CHAPTER 5
The Café

Arthur knew with certainty that he was the target of gossip at The Café.

"I'm finding that I miss The Café this morning, George."

"Yes, and I'm sure everyone at The Café is missing you, Arthur. As a matter of fact, I'm sure they are talking about nothing else."

"You're right." He rubbed a nervous tick over his left eye. "But they can talk all they want. If I don't tell them what's going on, they will never know," he said with the conviction of a judge.

"Considering this is Stones End, where everyone's secrets are eventually laid bare, I admire your confidence," said George.

Arthur bristled yet couldn't think of a stinging retort.

"At least, it's a weekday and I'm not missing Sunday breakfast."

Most villagers lined up for a "proper café breakfast" on Sunday morning. "You should expand and put more tables in," was the constant complaint to Oscar, the proprietor. "You got a hundred thousand dollars for a renovation?" he would ask in his usual curmudgeonly fashion justifying his nickname, *Oscar the Grump*.

Now if Oscar was known as *The Grump*, his wife, Madge, was known as *The Saint*, mostly because she put up with Oscar. It was a never-ending joke in Stones End.

They seemed the unlikeliest of couples. Oscar was a surly man who didn't suffer fools lightly while Madge was as cool as a cucumber and welcoming as Mother Earth on a spring day. Although it was an often source of discussion by villagers on what attracted Oscar and Madge to one another, the general consensus was, opposites really do attract. And stick together.

But despite Oscar's surliness, he was the best chef for a hundred miles around. Just good down-to-earth comfort food like meatloaf, Yankee pot roast, roast chicken and all served with creamy mashed potatoes, fresh roasted vegetables and at affordable prices.

But Thursday nights, ah, Thursday nights were special. Who could complain about the wait when the reward was something as delectable as roast duck with cherry sauce or lamb chops with mint jelly or grilled salmon with cranberry-pear vinaigrette?

Against vehement protests from Oscar, Madge insisted The Café be transformed into an elegant restaurant on Thursday nights.

"The place looks fine as it is. No one expects fancy," protested Oscar.

His protests fell on deaf ears. Madge always won.

She dressed each table with a white linen tablecloth and napkins. Small votive candles in etched glass holders, along with a fresh cut flower in a bud vase, adorned every table. The final touch of sparkle for The Café was white twinkle lights gracing the walls and front window.

The atmosphere in The Café was indeed transformed and villagers felt as though they were eating in a charming European bistro. They even dressed in their Sunday best to dine on a Thursday, no less.

"You outdid yourself, old girl, the place looks spectacular," he admitted.

"What did I forget, dear?"

"Nothing, Madge, absolutely nothing and don't spend another dime."

"No, no...it still needs something. Although for the life of me I can't think of what that is."

"Well, if anyone can figure it out, it's you. Just don't spend another dime."

"Oscar, we are investing in our future," said Madge, then yelled, "Music! That's what's missing, music."

So, Madge added music and had the brilliant idea that the menu offering should drive the choice. There was Italian music for saltimbocca, Greek music for roast lamb, Spanish music for paella, and more.

"Positively genius, Madge. How much did it cost?" *Oscar the Grump* couldn't help being grumpy.

CHAPTER 6
Martin, The Quiet Observer

Who *is this now?* thought Arthur at the sound of more footsteps. *I can't even enjoy my day off.*

"Don't complain, Arthur. It gives you more time to procrastinate about opening the letter."

"For heaven's sake, George, will you stop bringing up that bloody letter?"

Charging around the bend was Martin, Arthur's apprentice.

Martin was a young man of 20 with nervous youthful energy and was positively beside himself because Arthur had not been there to open the shop.

"My word," said Martin. "I thought you were dead!"

Just like Martin to think the worst, thought Arthur. *A classic overreactor.*

Martin always spoke with old English phrases like, "My word" or "Egad." Apparently, during an eighth-grade reading assignment of Charles Dickens, he fell in love with Victorian England. His love for the period grew so intense that he set a goal of saving enough money for a trip to the English countryside. He was sure he would love it there and may never return.

To complete his immersion into everything Victorian, Martin always wore a starched white high-collared shirt, complete with bowtie, suspendered trousers and a tweed jacket with leather elbow patches and, of course, he never went anywhere without his umbrella. His bumbershoot.

Martin's eccentricity was viewed as charming by some and irritating by others. But in the end, he was a most likable young fellow.

He did, however, possess the unnerving habit of being overly-observant. Martin simply noticed everything that went on in Stones End.

He had the uncanny ability to recall the most obscure details of conversations or happenings from years gone by. This dismayed some villagers who preferred to forget certain events. Caroline, the deputy sheriff, simply stated at one of the village gatherings, "That kid gives me the creeps."

❀ ❀

"I'm not dead, Martin. No need for such fussing."

"But the shop, it's not open!"

"So, open it, lad. You have the key."

"By Jove, you're right. I must confess, I didn't think of that. Please forgive the intrusion."

But as Martin turned to go, it struck him that Arthur had no intention of following. This was entirely unsettling to him. "Are you not well, sir?"

"I'm fine, Martin, just tired," Arthur said. George whispered, "Another lie."

Then the unthinkable happened. Before he could stop himself and giving no thought to the catastrophic consequences, the words spilled out of Arthur's mouth, "I'm taking a day off."

He immediately wanted to snatch them back for Arthur knew all too well they would set off what would feel like a nuclear explosion in the village.

Well, you could have knocked Martin over with a feather. *I may swoon,* he thought. *Better not, you don't have your smelling salts.*

Poor Martin simply turned and went off to open the shop wondering, *I bet that letter on Arthur's kitchen table has something to do with this.*

CHAPTER 7
The Nuclear Explosion

The word in the village would spread fast. Mrs. Kruchinski, the primary village gossip, would see to that. So, when Martin burst into the bakery and told her that Arthur was taking a day off, she almost popped.

No one knew how, but Mrs. Kruchinski was usually the first to know everything that happened in the village. She was known to start every gem of gossip with the phrase, "I got news!" This was always said with an urgent, hushed tone as if she didn't want anyone else to hear. Of course, it was laughable since all gossip spread faster than Road Runner being chased by Wile E. Coyote.

But this morning when Berris, the owner of the beauty parlor next door, came in for her usual double cappuccino and chocolate babka, Mrs. Kruchinski announced, "I got big news!"

This breach from the "Mrs. Kruchinski Book of Gossip Etiquette" caused Berris to drop her chocolate babka to the tile.

"Who died?"

"No one is dead!" Mrs. Kruchinski said dramatically waving her arm. "Bigger than that!"

"Bigger than that," said Berris. Her eyes were as big as saucers. "Lordy, don't keep me guessing. What is it?"

"ARTHUR...IS TAKING...A DAY...OFF!"

The news clearly shook Berris. She just stood there, not moving, not even blinking. There was a puzzled look on her face as though she just couldn't wrap her head around the news. The three things in life you could count on were death, taxes and Arthur working at the printshop six days a week. He worked during blizzards, ice storms, floods. Taking a day off, never!

"Big news, right?" said Mrs. Kruchinski.

"Big isn't the word. It's positively monumental! So, what's he doing on his day off?"

"Who's to say? He was just sitting on that bench of his."

CHAPTER 8
Berris, Master of All Things Colorful

Berris was a simple, uncomplicated soul who didn't like change. When she opened her shop, it was fashionable to call it a beauty parlor, but that was 20 years ago. Everyone told her time and again that they were now called hair salons. Berris' standard reply was that she liked the old-fashioned moniker of beauty parlor. "It sounds more charming," she said. But everyone knew she simply was incapable of change.

Even though Berris could not embrace personal change, she was always trying to get her customers to keep up with the times.

She considered herself quite a fashion maven but truth be told, she dressed with a lot of psychedelic everything. So, a fashion maven she was not...since 1968.

Her current endeavor was spray-in hair color which caused Berris to show up each morning with different color hair. Today's look was neon orange which made Mrs. Kruchinski wince. *Too much bright color so early in the morning.*

Berris' only success with her spray-in color venture was getting Constance Whitestead from the bookshop to try cobalt blue.

Now Mrs. Whitestead was a spunky, stylish English lady, but a proper one, and a shock of silver hair which made her a most unlikely guinea pig. So, when the new look did not go over well in the village, Mrs. Whitestead ran home in the middle of the day and washed it out. She was profoundly disappointed because secretly she liked the new look. And was dying to try bright pink next.

❧ ❧

"What do you mean he was just sitting there? Is he sick?"

"No, he's not sick. He said he's tired."

"Tired! What the heck is that supposed to mean? We're all tired."

"He says no, but I think he's sick," said Mrs. Kruchinski.

"Or maybe he's losing his marbles. He's no spring chicken, you know. How old do you think Arthur is, anyway?"

Now Mrs. Kruchinski and Arthur were the same age. She thought of herself in the prime of her life and still a force to be reckoned with. So, with a dramatic roll of her eyes, she said, "He's as old as I am. So, too young to be losing his marbles."

"Oh no, here comes Birdie," said Berris. "I didn't attend the meeting this week, who is she today?"

"Indira Gandhi," said Mrs. Kruchinski.

"Look at that, she's wearing a sari. I definitely should have guessed Indira. What do you think she will make of Arthur not going to work today?"

"I don't think Indira ever met Arthur. So, I'm guessing she won't care."

CHAPTER 9
Adapting to the Plan

"So, how is your diversion plan going?"

"It's going to take some getting used to, George. Maybe, I should just pop down to The Café for a quick cup."

"You've already had two."

"Well then, I could pick up a newspaper."

"Now Arthur, you know very well, if you set one foot in The Café, the talk will quickly turn to why you are taking a day off. Mrs. Kruchinski will interrogate you."

Arthur's jaw tightened at the thought of being grilled by Mrs. Kruchinski.

"You're absolutely right, George. If anyone can get you to spill your guts, it's Olga Kruchinski."

"Best to just stay put. Besides, you have a lot of thinking to get through today and a decision to make."

"By the way, Arthur, does anyone in the village know your story?"

"Not entirely. There was a night long ago when Birdie Hissop and I were the last to leave an event. She was pretty drunk."

"And that's saying something. I hear Birdie can drink a pirate under the table."

Arthur let out a belly laugh. "True enough, George. But the drink got the better of her this particular night. She started telling me some of her own tragic story and I talked a little about mine."

"So, someone actually knows your story."

"Not really. Neither one of us went into detail. We just sort of talked around the edges. I believe her memory is as painful as mine and she couldn't bring herself to relate the full account."

"Maybe you can ask her advice on what...."

"Absolutely not, George. The reason for not telling Birdie still exists. I haven't shared my story with another living soul. And that's the way I want it."

"I was just thinking you could use a little help with sorting your situation out, that's all."

"You're making too much of this, George," said Arthur slamming his hand down. "I'm either going to open the letter or I'm not. Either way is not the end of the world. And I'm sure I can figure this out on my own. Thank you very much."

"You poor, delusional man," said George. "Arthur, you are at a crossroad. This is big. You know it and I know it. Just face this dilemma in your usual head-on fashion and get on with life."

"I don't need your tough love, George. Just drop it, please."

Arthur didn't know how to face his past, much less resolve the issues it created.

Is it possible George was right? Maybe I should talk to someone. But who?

CHAPTER 10
History for Dummies

Birdie always coveted the position of head of the Village Historical Society and threw her name in the hat as a nominee when the job became available.

Mrs. Kruchinski thought it should be held by someone dignified.

"Birdie Hissop is a lot of things, my friends, but dignified isn't one of them."

Despite Mrs. Kruchinski's vehement concerns, Birdie won the day and the appointment with a unanimous vote. An ongoing thorn in Mrs. Kruchinski's side.

Birdie immediately rallied. At the first village meeting, she announced her plans for creating a mission for the society. She'd reveal them at the next meeting.

"Oh boy," said Mrs. Kruchinski, "this is going to be a dilly."

Birdie spent the week before the meeting putting up countdown posters all over the village.

Seven Days to: "The Big History Reveal"

Six Days to: "Everything you wanted to know about history, but were afraid to ask"

Five Days to: "The past leads to our future"

Finally, the big day arrived. The village hall was packed.

When all were seated, Birdie had Martin cut the lights.

As the villagers sat in darkness, they heard someone walk onto the stage. When Birdie was in position, she yelled, "Hit it, Martin!" A spotlight lit center stage. There stood Birdie dressed like George Washington complete with a white powdered wig.

And with great theatrical flair, Birdie announced that the society's mission was raising everyone's awareness of historic world leaders.

Her plan consisted of weekly presentations and then it got weird, as Mrs. Kruchinski said. For the second part of Birdie's plan was to take on the character of the world leader for the week. This included dressing and talking like them.

Villagers considered Birdie's plan crazy, yet they did enjoy Pocahontas Week when Birdie dressed as an American Indian complete with bow and arrow.

Someone made the mistake of commenting they didn't actually consider Pocahontas a world leader. Birdie whacked him in the arm. "I like the costume."

After Pocahontas Week, Mrs. Kruchinski bitterly regretted appointing Birdie Hissop as village historian and vowed to get her removed.

CHAPTER 11
Routine in Tatters

"I lied today, George. I don't think I've ever lied in my entire life. And it's not even 8 in the morning and I've told two lies already. I shudder to think what else this day holds. Something very strange is happening and don't say it's the letter."

"I didn't say a thing," but Arthur knew George was thinking it.

He went into the house and made a third cup of coffee. *My routine is in tatters,* he thought.

As he leaned against the counter waiting for his brew, he looked at the unopened letter on the kitchen table. The letter, he knew, was the source of his lies and he could barely set his eyes on it for more than a moment. It sat there screaming, *OPEN ME,* but Arthur was simply not ready to discover its contents. *George is right. I'm in total denial.*

Arthur was no sooner back on the porch when George asked, "What are you afraid of? It's just a letter."

"Getting right to the core of it?"

"Well, if I don't, then that bloody letter will never get opened."

Arthur felt a crack in the dam holding back his memories. Suddenly, an urgent need to lift some of his burden caused him to blurt out, "I'm ashamed of something I did in my past, George. And I've been running from the memory of it my whole life."

"Everyone has some sore spot in their life. You and I have sat out here with most of the residents of Stones End. Some come because they're lonely, some come to just say hello, but sooner or later, all come to unload a burden."

"It's not the same thing, George."

"I know it isn't. But did you ever notice everyone leaves feeling lighter, feeling relieved? Confront what's bothering you and be done with it. If you don't face your fears, they'll never go away."

"I'm afraid this one will never go away, George. You see, I let someone down and you can't take that back. I abandoned someone. Someone I love dearly. And it has left me with a question I have not been able to answer my whole life."

"How can that be? You've never let anyone down. And what is this burning question, anyway?"

"Not sure it matters any longer. She went on to have a wonderful life without me. But what's been eating at me for the past 40 years is why didn't I fight for the woman I loved? At the first sign of trouble, I ran away. I had my reasons at the time and they seemed warranted, even noble."

"I have no doubt they were."

"I had a chance to stand and fight or run and I chose to run. What kind of man does that?"

"I have to admit it doesn't sound like you. But, Arthur, I know you and I am positive of one thing, if you left, then it was the right decision. You just haven't figured it out yet but you will. Maybe what's in the letter will give you the answer."

"I think I know the answer, George. I ran away because I was afraid. So that makes me a coward as well as a heel."

"Arthur, a person's lowest moment does not define who they are. Life is made up of a million moments. And the sum of yours makes you an honorable man whose moral compass is always pointing north."

"Nice of you to say. But you may be a little biased."

"We all make mistakes, Arthur, but there is always forgiveness and redemption for everyone. Maybe that's what the letter is offering you."

"Maybe it is, George, but I don't think I deserve it."

"You're wrong, Arthur. Never refuse forgiveness and the redemption it offers. Never."

"And what if the letter doesn't offer forgiveness?"

"You've lived without her forgiveness this long. Why is it so important now?"

Arthur sat with his thoughts which was always a safe place to be. In his mind, he could imagine not being forgiven. But thoughts could be shut out.

He was tired of thinking. George was landing one gut punch after another and it was wearing on him. He needed to relax.

Closing his eyes, he let the soothing sound of the rushing river calm his jittering nerves. He inhaled the scent of damp pine needles and felt the warmth of the sun gently touching his face.

Suddenly, he was overwhelmed with a feeling that she was by his side. His senses were transferring to her presence. The sound of the rushing river was now her musical voice, the sweet smell of pine, her perfume and the sun's warm touch, her hand tenderly caressing his face.

His spell was broken by the screech from an angry crow. Arthur's body jerked abruptly returning him fully to his pressing issue.

If the letter spoke words of condemnation, then not being forgiven would become reality.

What would happen to my memories? They would slip away, he thought. *As though they never existed. And I'd be left with the realization that I'm just an old fool who wasted his life in the shadow of a dream.*

Arthur breathed a long and labored sigh. "Let it be, George. Just let it be."

Don't give up, Arthur. Don't you dare give up. I'll see you safely to the other side.

CHAPTER 12
Call to Action

Berris picked up her cappuccino and babka and headed for the door.

"I've got to go. Esther Lubbitz is coming in at 8 for a pedicure and I need time to mentally prepare."

"How are her bunions?"

"Don't ask," said Berris.

As she turned to go, she stopped and looked at Mrs. Kruchinski, who was staring out beyond the shop window.

"What are we going to do about Arthur, Mrs. K? I'm worried about him."

Mrs. Kruchinski snapped her head toward Berris as though hit by a lightning bolt.

"We need to call an emergency council meeting, Berris. That's what we need to do. You are absolutely right. Something bad is going on with Arthur and we need to get to the bottom of it."

"Go over to The Café and tell Madge that Arthur is taking a day off and no one knows why. Then tell her that there is an emergency meeting at 9 to figure out what's going on."

Completely charged with her urgent task, Berris shouted over her shoulder as she ran out, "I'll certainly do that, Mrs. K."

Berris burst through The Café door and yelled to Madge, "Mrs. K is calling an emergency meeting at 9."

"What now?" asked Walter over a bowl of leaden oatmeal. "Did someone leave another soda can in front of the bakery?"

"No, there's something terribly wrong with Arthur."

"What?" said Madge almost dropping a stack of dirty plates. "Is he alright?"

"No one knows. He didn't go to work today. He's just sitting up there with George not doing anything."

Chairs overturned as everyone made a mad rush to the counter to hear the gossip.

"Didn't go to work today!" Madge said. "Wait till Oscar hears this."

"Where is Oscar? He and Arthur are good friends. Maybe he knows what's wrong," said Birdie.

"It's market day. He should be back soon."

"I don't ever remember Arthur taking a day off," said old Horace, the mail carrier.

"It's a first," said Birdie. "And I've known Arthur 40 years."

"I've gotta run but I'll be back for the meeting," said Berris. But as she moved toward the door, she turned back and said, "I sure hope we can figure out how to help Arthur. I'm kinda worried."

"We may be overreacting, folks," said Walter. "It could be something as innocent as Arthur needs a day off after 40 years. It is, after all, a very long time."

31

They all turned and looked at Walter as though he had monkeys crawling out of his ears.

"Funny, he doesn't look stupid," Birdie said.

Walter relented under the pressure of all the glaring eyes. "Or maybe there's something terribly, terribly wrong with Arthur. In any case, I'll be back for the meeting." He grabbed his newspaper and headed for the door.

"Me too," said Birdie. "Arthur taking a day off. Never thought I'd see the day."

"I hope it's not a health issue," Horace said, swinging his mail sack over his shoulder.

Martin sat quietly through the frantic scene. He thought, *Arthur can be as stubborn as the day is long. I surely hope George can get him to do the right thing.*

CHAPTER 13
Bittersweet Memories

The first sliver of sun was slowly climbing over the horizon and Arthur realized he hadn't sat and watched a full sunrise since that last summer he worked with his father.

"Now this is more like it," Arthur said to George. "I should take a day off more often."

It had rained the night before and the scent of wet dirt hung heavily in the air. When the light hit the dew-laden branches, every twig, branch and leaf sparkled as though it held precious jewels as its bounty. The shimmering beauty not only took Arthur's breath away but jarred strong memories from his youth.

Each summer when school let out, Arthur went to work at his father's boatyard. The boatyard was an integral part of the tiny Greek village where he lived.

Fishing was the mainstay in Corso and dominated conversation among the men. The women of Corso, however, talked incessantly about their children, when they were not sharing fish recipes, that is.

It seemed to Arthur they ate fish morning, noon and night. They ate fish and rice (Psaropilafo Tis Kivelis), fish soup (Soupyes & Spanaki), fish in garlic sauce (Bakaliaros). But fish is what they had, so, fish is what they ate and no one thought to complain.

Theirs was a meager existence and the women shared just about everything as a means of survival.

"Christine," Mrs. Stavros, called out to her neighbor. "Has your Nicky moved to a bed yet?"

"Yes. Why do you ask?"

"Because Margot's daughter is about to give birth and needs a crib."

"Yes, of course. Tell her husband to stop by anytime."

Corso women also shared their children's clothes. When one child grew out of them, they were given to another child that size. Arthur remembered not wearing a new garment till he went to work and could afford a store-bought shirt and pants.

The village was nestled in a cove that opened to the Mediterranean Sea. It consisted of a dozen or so shops, one restaurant and a local bar called The Black Pearl where the fishermen ended each day before heading home.

The Black Pearl was what Arthur called a "man's bar" decorated with sawdust floors, boat and fish pictures and roughly-hewn pine tables. The stench of beer, fish and sweat greeted patrons at the door as did the din of salty language that would make a nun's ears bleed.

Although Corso had a rundown appearance, it was a pretty little village. The shopkeepers took great pride in their establishments, keeping their windows and sidewalks scrubbed clean. "We may be poor," said Mrs. Pappas, "but that doesn't mean we have to be dirty."

All the shops sat on one side of the main street. A park across the road was lined with benches offering a view of unparalleled beauty of the sea just beyond. Blue-green sparkling water, luminous white houses on a jutting peninsula and warm, gentle breezes.

The jewel of the crown in Corso was St. Gregory's Church. It was a small stone church adorned with four magnificent stained-glass windows donated by the rich folks who lived on seaside estates outside the village.

Arthur's strongest memory of home was that the smell of salty sea air was forever fighting the greasy stench of fried fish.

Unwelcome Changes

Every day, Arthur and his father arrived at the boatyard just before dawn to witness the flurry of activity as the fishermen made ready their boats and nets before setting out to sea for a day or longer.

Once the small fleet set sail, Arthur and his father would sit in awe as the sun made its daily journey over the horizon. They never tired of seeing the string of fishing boats silhouetted in the warm coral glow of the early-morning light.

Arthur cherished their morning routine for it was the only quiet time he got to spend with his father.

Arthur's father was a patient, gentle man. He was tall, with lean sinewy strength that impressed even the stockiest of fishermen. His stick-straight hair already showed strands of grey and it was a constant source of annoyance that it forever fell in his eyes. He threatened many a time to get one of those new cuts the kids were sporting but his wife, Helena, loved his hair long and forbid him to cut it.

His father was always taking time to impart some favorite pearl of wisdom to his son. "Let go of the day's worries each night so there's room for tomorrow's joys." Another: "Don't ever trust your heart, Arthur, always go with your gut; for your heart is fickle and your gut is true."

Hailed as a master carpenter, his father set his skills to boat-building, fishing boats to be exact. He sold the odd boat now and again but mostly the fishermen relied on his keen eye and expert skills to do whatever it took to keep their vessels seaworthy.

Each evening, Arthur's father would stand at the water's edge and watch the fleet return. He'd look for sails that weren't catching the full wind, listen for the slightest ping of a finicky diesel, take note of masts that weren't standing straight. And Arthur's father could spot a pinprick of wood rot from 50 paces. Yes, he took seriously keeping the ragtag little fleet on the high seas.

The boatyard provided Arthur's family a modest lifestyle. It was what most people called poor, actually, except Arthur's mother who called their status *low middle income.* She was known to call the boatyard a shipyard and told everyone her husband was a shipbuilder.

This bothered Arthur. *She doesn't know what's important in life.* What his father provided was never enough for his mother. His father only chuckled at her exaggerations.

It was his father's secret wish that one day he would train Arthur to take over the boatyard. His mother had other plans. Her husband's brother owned a printshop in the village and she insisted that Arthur work there starting next summer.

Helena approached her husband to set the wheels in motion for Arthur's future.

"Arthur will be 18 next year and high time he learned a formal trade, where he'll only come home with ink on his hands and not the smell of the fish guts he's cleaned off the decks."

Next summer, Arthur found himself working for his Uncle Charlie at the printshop. It would be useless, he knew, raging against this unwanted change.

The bitter resentment he harbored made him miss, all the more, working with his father. And the staff at the printshop seemed a dull lot compared to the raucous comradery of the boat captains and their crews.

But soon, his love of crafting teak decks was replaced with a love of crafting editorial copy for the presses. And in the end, the thrill of beating deadlines won over the monotony of mending nets.

It was thrilling to Arthur that the shop was hired to print the local and regional newspapers. The regional paper included world events and the flood of knowledge beyond his limited world fed his adventurous spirit.

Arthur enjoyed getting to know the professional side of Uncle Charlie and found his passion for the printing business matched his father's passion for wood. There was no doubt that his father's blood reeked with the sweet smell of cedar and his uncle's blood ran black as the ink on his presses.

His father often got paid with the catch of the day and to-day's catch was sea bass or lavraki as the locals knew it. His mother prepared the sea bass in the traditional Greek method of stuffing the stomach with garlic and herbs and baking it in a grease-proof paper with fresh tomatoes. It was a family favorite.

Arthur would bring the news of the day home to discuss around the dinner table. He always started with local news which he felt paled in comparison to the wondrous events taking place on the global stage. But his parents only were interested in their village news and could care less about world events.

"There was a fire in Mrs. Stavropoulos' kitchen today," Arthur announced.

"Oh my goodness," his mother said, quickly making the sign of the cross.

"And it looks like the United States Congress is calling for President Nixon's impeachment."

"Was there much damage to her kitchen?" asked his mother.

"No, hardly any damage." But before Arthur could steer back to world events, he was thwarted by his father.

"Ari, are you going into the city any time soon? There are some new tools I need."

"Sure, Pop. On Thursday, just give me your list."

"I still say you're too young to be traveling into the city alone, Aristotle," his mother fretted.

"I'll be fine, Mom. And, in case you haven't noticed, I'm 22 years old."

"It's just that I worry when my children are out of sight, that's all."

"Where's Emily tonight?" asked their father.

"She has a date," replied Zoe, taking great satisfaction in sharing Emily's secret.

"A date! With whom?" asked his mother charging across the room like an angry bull. "She told me she was going to the movies with a friend."

"She is with a friend and his name is Stephen."

"Zoe," Arthur said, "you weren't supposed to tell."

"You knew as well, Arthur? And you didn't tell your mother and me?" His voice was on the rise as was his blood pressure.

Seeing the rise of color in his father's face, Arthur tried to steady his anger. "Stephen is a nice guy, Pop. He works at the printshop with me. You and Mom would like him."

"Maybe we would if Emily had given us the opportunity to meet him," his father said stiffly.

"Things are different today, Pop," said Ari. "It's much more relaxed than when you and Mom were dating. And, by the way, Emily is 21 now. I'd think that's old enough to go on a date without permission."

"Relaxed, you say." The dishes jumped as he slammed his hand to the table. "Not in this house! In this house, daughters respect their parents and bring their dates home to meet the family."

The air was sucked out of the room by his father's rage. Arthur chanced a glance in his direction fully expecting to see anger written on the lines of his face. But it wasn't anger he saw. It was fear.

It suddenly occurred to Arthur how hard his parents were fighting against the violent changing of the times. Casual sex. Drug use. And the melancholy lyrics of their beloved Greek music replaced by revolutionary chants. It scared them to death.

So much for discussing world events, thought Arthur.

Dinner ended abruptly. Arthur, Aristotle and Zoe knew to make themselves invisible. They ran from the house.

"Zoe, what the heck were you thinking telling Mom and Pop about Emily's date?" Arthur spat out.

"I know. I regret it now. Pop's so mad. But she borrowed my new dress without permission and I wanted to get back at her."

"I don't think I've ever seen Pop so angry," said Aristotle.

"I have," said Arthur. "I wasn't paying attention to what I was doing with the boat lift one day and almost dropped the schooner on my head. Pop was both mad and scared."

"You? Mr. Careful, making a mistake like that. Can't imagine it."

"Give me a break. I was only 16 at the time."

At the mention of the schooner, Arthur's thoughts made a welcome departure from the family drama. He was suddenly back in the boatyard putting the finishing touches on the great schooner.

A Labor of Love

For all the years he worked with his father, his job was to mend the fishing nets and whenever he finished early, Arthur would help his father with the boat repairs. He was amazed at how complicated some of the repairs were and marveled at his father's masterful skills.

His father was thrilled with Arthur's carpentry. "He understands the wood," he would tell his wife. "That's a rare gift."

So, at the beginning of that last summer, his father proudly announced that Arthur would take over the boat repairs and he would mend the nets.

"Are you sure, Pop?" Arthur said in a stunned voice.

"Yes, son, you're more than ready. And, not to worry, I'm always here."

"Don't worry, Pop, I won't let you down."

Now there was a grand old schooner in the boatyard that suffered considerable damage during a violent storm. The schooner was entering the cove when a gale-force wind ripped the air crashing it into the rocks guarding the narrow channel.

The once-magnificent schooner looked piteous laying on its side. Mast broken in two, teak deck hideously twisted and buckled, shredded sails and a gaping hole large enough for a grown man to walk through on her port side.

Despite knowing he was lucky to have survived, the owner's superstitions took hold. "Bad luck," was all he said before he walked away from the shore.

But good luck for Arthur's father who loved the schooner. He and Arthur spent two days hauling it off the rocks and into the boatyard.

She was a 50-footer fashioned of solid teak with a commanding wheelhouse and two cabins with galley, head and bunks below.

Arthur saw how much his father loved the schooner. He'd spend a few spare hours working on it but never making much progress.

Then one day he announced, "Pop, you and I are going to put this boat back together. I'll come after school and all day on weekends. And when we're finished, we are going to take her for the ride of our lives. Maybe Italy. Croatia!"

The damage to the schooner appeared insurmountable. They would have to rebuild the shattered hull, replace more than half the teak deck, and the cost to replace the oak mast would eat up two months of wages and that was just for starters. He didn't want to disappoint his son but hope seemed a luxury of the youth.

Arthur persisted. Seeing the determination on his face, the youthful hope, the pleading in his eyes for him to say yes, Arthur's father felt a hope of his own growing. A hope he hadn't felt in a very long time.

And without any thought of how they would accomplish such a daunting task, he answered, "Yes, my boy, yes. Let's put her back together." Making that simple pledge to his youngest son kindled energy. They couldn't wait to get started.

Soon word got out that Arthur and his father were planning to repair the old schooner and the news breathed new life into the tired little village itself.

Before they knew it, lumber appeared mysteriously in the boatyard each morning. Arthur and his father marveled at the generosity of their neighbors.

"We're fortunate, Arthur, very fortunate to have such wonderful friends." He vowed to take them all for a sail when the schooner was finished.

Arthur's mother was not happy. She worried that her overworked husband was taking on too much. *She ruins everything,* thought Arthur. He was angry with her for throwing a wet blanket over their dream.

"My dear husband, you have me worried to death with this boat thing."

"Helena, you worry too much. I'm fine."

"You don't have time for this," Helena pleaded. "You were already working six days a week and now you're working seven. It's too much."

"Please don't worry, my love. This project has breathed new life into these old bones and is making me feel quite youthful again. The spring is back in my step."

Helena was surprised to see that he did, indeed, look ten years younger. There was an excitement about him that was contagious.

"Fine, my dearest, I'll stop nagging. You do actually look like a new man but if this boat thing kills you, don't come complaining to me."

"I love you, my dear."

"I love you more."

Every weekend and whatever time they could find during the week, Arthur and his father worked on the schooner.

Rebuilding the hull took forever. Long planks of wood had to be soaked, steamed and shaped and there was no hurrying the process. The massive amount of patchwork on the deck was equally time-consuming. Removing the destroyed sections without damaging what was still intact proved to be tedious work.

Arthur was often frustrated with how long the repairs were taking. It was at these times, his father would say, "Never hurry a job, my boy. Do it right or don't do it at all. A substandard job could cost a sailor his life on the high seas."

"You're right, Pop, especially considering we're the sailors now."

"Exactly," said his father smiling as he tussled Arthur's hair. "Always knew you were a bright lad."

Thereafter, Arthur kept his frustration in check. The repairs took two years. It was the best time of his life. It was a time when he came to understand the meaning of *a labor of love.*

And then the last summer he worked with his father, they made her seaworthy.

"We did it, Pop. She's finished!" Arthur said. "What are you going to name her?"

"There's only one name for her, Arthur. *The Helena,* after your mother."

The day before school started was to be *The Helena's* maiden voyage. Arthur couldn't sleep the night before, nor could his father.

They were up at the crack of dawn to face the long-awaited day.

"Perfect day for a sail," Arthur's father said slapping his son on the back.

"It certainly is, Pop!"

They grabbed their gear and headed for the boatyard.

To their surprise, the village was deserted. They had expected everyone to be calling out good wishes for the big day but all the shops were closed tight. Not a curtain moved on any of the windows betraying a nosy neighbor and even the church bells were suspiciously silent for a Sunday morning.

"It looks like a ghost town," Arthur said.

"It is strange. Come to think of it, where are your mother, brother and sisters this morning?"

"Still sleeping?"

"I don't think so, Arthur, your mother is up before me each morning."

As they reached the edge of town and started down the hill toward the boatyard, the mystery of the deserted village was solved.

The entire population of Corso was already gathered at the water's edge and Arthur and his father could feel the air crackling with excitement. A party for them.

"Pop, did you ever see the boatyard look so grand!"

Arthur's father clapped his hands together exclaiming, "It's going to be a great day, my boy!"

Brightly decorated tables and chairs transformed the waterfront. A blue and white striped canvas tent housed a banquet. Overflowing food tables held large bowls of lemon potatoes, platters of moussaka, stuffed grape leaves, shaved lamb slices, spanokopita.

Father Giorgos got help carrying the Madonna and Child

statue on a platform to place at the water's edge. A rainbow of streamers and banners and balloons could have lifted every chair, table and umbrella.

The dilapidated, old boatyard had the look of a lively festival and the villagers came to celebrate the father and son who breathed new life into their wanting lives and *The Helena*.

Everyone waged their plea to go on the maiden voyage but Arthur's father reserved the first sail for him and Arthur alone.

But first, the schooner had to be blessed and christened. All heads dropped as Father Giorgos prayed for safe voyages on the high seas.

Then namesake Helena stepped onto the platform. Arthur's mother looked nervous. She was wringing her hands and barely gave up a smile to her friends.

The mayor donated a bottle of champagne for the momentous occasion. With bottle in hand, his mother announced in a very loud and proud voice, "I hereby christen thee, *The Helena*."

The bottle shattered. The crowd erupted. Cheers, whistles and applause burst into the air with Arthur's father and siblings screeching the loudest.

Finally, the schooner was launched into the water causing another great roar of excitement. And then the moment Arthur and his father had been waiting for these two long years.

They climbed the ladder onto the deck and set their sails. And as the mighty schooner cleared the cove, they were sent off to sea with wild cheers, waving arms and joyful dancing.

Arthur was sure he would burst from the sheer joy of the

moment. It was the most thrilling day of his life. Just he and his father with the wind in their faces, the quiet power of the vast sea and not a care in the world.

As they cleared the cove on their return, a tearful Arthur quietly said, "I'll never forget this day, Pop, not ever."

"Nor I, son," his father said displaying his broadest grin. "Thank you for making this dream of mine come true. I couldn't have done it without you."

Arthur was overwhelmed with pride. "The best day ever!"

❧❧

"I loved that schooner, George."

"Must be one of your favorite memories, Arthur. You've re-lived it many times with me."

"Shame we didn't get to use it more. But it wasn't too long before...."

Arthur tried to stop his thoughts knowing the painful memories the following summer held. His mind heartlessly dragged him forward.

Darkness Falls

Now Arthur's father couldn't afford to pay him. The little money Arthur earned during the summer came from what the fishermen paid him for scraping and scrubbing the fish guts off their decks at the end of the day.

So, when Arthur went to work for his uncle the following year, his father had to cover the extra tasks himself. He almost drowned in work.

This concerned Arthur who helped his father each night after his day at the printshop.

One day, a rush job caused Arthur to work late. He was so tired, he went directly home. When he saw his father wasn't there, he checked with his mother.

"He's working late, as always."

It was much later than his father's usual time and Arthur was worried. "I'll go see if Pop needs a hand."

"He's fine, Arthur. Go sit and have your supper." Still, Arthur headed out.

He was sure he would meet his father coming up from the boatyard but as he got closer and still didn't see him, panic set in. He began to run.

He reached the boatyard out of breath. "Pop, you here?" His father didn't answer. He first checked the office, the garage and then began frantically calling out. "Pop, where are you?"

He stopped dead in his tracks.

His father's arm was sticking up from the side of one of the dry-docked boats. Arthur's heart was pounding.

He flew up the ladder onto the deck. There lay his father, his hammer by his side where it dropped.

"Pop, are you alright?" Arthur yelled. His father opened his eyes and gave a weak smile. Arthur imagined the worst. "I'll get help."

"No, Arthur, don't leave me," his father quietly said.

He pulled his father onto his lap and cradled his head. Tears raced down Arthur's face. *Please don't die,* echoed in his head.

"I should have never taken the job at the printshop," Arthur choked out. "I should have been here working with you, Pop. Why did Mom make me leave you when you needed me?"

"No, son," his father said in a thin voice, "your mother rightfully wanted something better for you. We both did."

"But she always wanted more than you could give us, Pop."

His father's breathing was ragged. His voice raspy.

"We all have a right to dream. But make no mistake," he tried to catch his breath. "Your mother was always grateful for what she had."

Violent coughing consumed him. Arthur's heart broke as he witnessed his father fight to live just a few moments more.

His voice turned weaker.

"She was a good wife to me, Arthur...." His chest was heaving. "And a wonderful mother to you children," he whispered in the past tense as if he were already gone.

Arthur gripped tighter. Suddenly, his father closed his eyes. Arthur held his breath waiting for some movement. None came. He shook his father and desperately screamed, "Pop, are you still with me?"

Arthur's father slowly opened his eyes and waved his hand slightly for Arthur to come closer.

"Thank you, my son...you have made me so proud."

His eyes closed again. Arthur could barely hear his words.

"More than I deserve."

His father's chest was rattling. Arthur waited in agony.

"Promise me...you'll take care of your mother."

And with his last drop of strength, his father opened his eyes willing himself to live until the answer. Arthur nodded.

"I'll take care of her, Pop. I promise. I won't let you down."

The thin veil separating life from death lifted. Arthur's father closed his eyes, gave up the good fight and died in Arthur's arms.

A Powerful Emotion

Now, anger is a powerful emotion. So powerful, it caused Arthur to forget his promise to his father.

They say all anger needs someone to blame. Some blame themselves. Some blame God. Arthur blamed his mother for his father's death.

His hurt and anger were so great, he couldn't be moved to speak to her. His mother pleaded with Arthur to tell her what was wrong but he simply refused to answer.

He saw his mother as someone who never appreciated his father and always made him feel as though he was not good enough. And Arthur believed deep down in his heart that she put his father in an early grave.

And there was no forgiveness for that, not now, not ever.

After the funeral, Arthur packed his belongings and went to live with his father's brother. His Uncle Charlie begged Arthur to go home to his mother in her time of need.

"No, Uncle. She doesn't need me. She doesn't need anyone."

In the weeks afterward, Arthur focused on printing so he wouldn't go mad with grief.

There was the boatyard to deal with so he called a meeting with his older brother and sisters, Aristotle, Zoe and Emily to talk about what to do.

"I think we should keep the boatyard open," Arthur started. "I know we all have full-time jobs and I don't want it to become a burden. But Pop's passion lives on in that tired old yard. I would hate to let that go. I'm sure if we put our heads together, we can come up with a way to keep it going."

Zoe looked as though she was going to explode. "I have been wanting to expand Pop's business for years! We can use the schooner for fishing charters for tourists."

"And the small boat that Pop never sold could be used to ferry tourists around our islands," said Emily enthusiastically.

"And vacations," added Aristotle. "People could charter the schooner to sail the Mediterranean for a week."

"Outstanding ideas," said Arthur clapping his hands together loudly.

Zoe was excellent with numbers and offered to keep the books. She would still work at the bank during the week and at the boatyard on the weekends, and nights, if necessary.

Arthur wanted to stay at the printshop and would work in the evenings and every weekend at the boatyard.

And Aristotle had already worked out who they could hire to help with repairs and net mending. He would oversee the daily workers and be the PR and front-desk man because of his gift of gab. They all laughed at this but knew it was true.

Excitement for the future filled them. *Pop would be so pleased,* Arthur thought. And the siblings embraced one another enormously pleased for the opportunity to keep their beloved father's legacy alive.

Since Arthur was still not speaking with his mother, he left it up to his siblings to inform her. Because the boatyard was left to her, they needed her approval which they all knew she would give.

Forgiveness and Redemption

It was exactly one month after the meeting when Arthur saw his uncle take an urgent call in his office. Uncle Charlie dropped the phone and ran out of the shop. Arthur had never seen him so distressed and started to worry.

It was mid-afternoon when someone handed Arthur a message: *Come home immediately.* He ran all the way.

His uncle and siblings were in the parlor. Zoe ran to him, "Mama's dead, Arthur. She's gone to be with Papa." And a heaviness pressed down on Arthur as he recalled his broken promises to his father.

He vaguely remembered hearing conversations in the background of how his father's death was just too much for his mother. Of how she loved him so much, she died of a broken heart at the thought of living without him.

Arthur's anxiety was mounting. His mother's death was his fault. His father's death was his fault.

Why didn't I help Pop more? Why didn't I go directly to the boatyard that night? Maybe I could have saved Pop. Why didn't I repair the tear in my relationship with Mom? Did it have anything to do with her death?

And the weight of these unanswered questions crushed him.

It was a long day of mourning. The final visit to the funeral home held a deep sadness. It was the last time they would see their mother. The emotion of the Mass drained them. Their hearts were heavy as they left St. Gregory's. And the finality of the graveside prayers was almost too much to bear. They were numb.

As Arthur stood at his mother's gravesite, the promises he made to his father echoed. *Don't worry, Pop, I'll never let you down. I'll take care of her, Pop, I promise.* An emotional dam broke. *But I did let you down, and you, too, Mom.*

Arthur's guilt blanketed his heart and soul until he could no longer hold its weight. Dropping to his knees at the sandy grave, he cried, "How could I do that? How could I break my promises?"

He sobbed uncontrollably. "I'm sorry Pop. I'm so sorry I let you down. You, too, Mom. Please forgive me."

Uncle Charlie cried out, "No, Arthur, don't do this." He ran to Arthur, wrapped his arms around his shoulders and guided him away from the gravesite.

"You didn't let them down, Arthur, you didn't let them down. They loved you and were proud of you always."

Friends and family gathered at his parents' house afterward. They ate and cried and hugged and cried and told stories about Helena.

"Your mother was a saint, Arthur," said Mrs. Stavros.

"All the work she did at the children's hospital and the church and nursing home. Don't know how Helena found the time," her best friend Elsie told everyone.

"Do you remember how she rallied the town when her husband and Arthur were putting the schooner back together? We all went into action finding wood. She swore us to secrecy. So, we brought our bits and pieces of oak, teak, cypress in the dark of night. It was great fun. We all felt like spies on a mission," said Mr. Pappas.

"There was never a person in need who your mother said no to, Arthur. She helped everyone," said Father Giorgos, as he made the sign of the cross. The room followed.

Arthur was not unlike most children who never notice all that their parents do. Sadly, for him, the revelation came too late. He would never get to know this side of his mother. *How did I not know any of this? How could I possibly miss all that my mother did for people? How many lives she made better.*

Arthur lowered his head. He shut his eyes tightly trying to hide from the raw shame he felt. The weight pushing on him made it hard for him to draw breath.

It was after 9 pm when Arthur said goodnight and trudged back to his uncle's house. He felt physically exhausted and emotionally empty. He could hardly walk or think.

Uncle Charlie left before Arthur and was waiting for him. As Arthur slammed the front door, he called out.

"Arthur, can you come into my study for a moment?"

"Uncle Charlie, can it wait? I'm done in."

"I'm afraid not, Arthur. This won't take long."

Uncle Charlie handed him an envelope. Arthur's name was written on the outside in his mother's handwriting.

"Your mother's friend, Elsie, brought it over this morning. Elsie said your mother knew she was dying for some time. She wrote a letter to each of her children before she passed. She asked Elsie to deliver yours right after the funeral."

Arthur stood staring at the letter. *A voice from the grave. What could Mom possibly have written?* His head felt woozy and he was sure if he didn't sit, he would topple over.

"Are you alright? Why don't you sit down, my boy?"

"I'm fine, Uncle Charlie. Just feeling a bit lightheaded."

He thanked his uncle and said he'd read the letter in his room. Uncle Charlie understood.

Arthur sat on the side of his bed looking down at the letter in his hands. He was surprised he felt nothing, not even curiosity. It was as if all emotion had been drained from him. He was empty. His mother was gone. His father was gone. He felt completely alone.

He laid his head on his pillow and fell asleep without opening the letter. Suddenly, he was treading water in a vast black sea. It was nighttime and he had no life jacket. He swam endlessly. His energy finally abandoned him. He was drowning in an angry sea of his emotions.

Arthur bolted straight up. An icy terror stabbed at him. The sweat of panic filled his nostrils. He didn't know where he was.

He saw the letter on the floor next to his bed. It was the only familiar thing in the room and he grabbed onto it as if it were the life preserver he needed to stay alive. He ripped open the envelope and began to read.

❧·❧

My precious son,

When you read this letter, I will be with your father in heaven.

I am so sad to leave my children, especially you, because we didn't get a chance to patch things up between us.

Now you didn't tell me and I wasn't there to hear it, but I know your father better than I know my own self. So, I know his last words would have been for you to take care of me.

Your old mother knows you, too, Arthur. You're going to think you let your father down. Please let these feelings go, my son. They will only take the joy out of your life.

It was just our time to go and it's nobody's fault. And neither your father nor I left this good Earth feeling cheated. Ours was a rich life full of love.

It's a funny thing, you children always thought I wore the pants in the family and that all decisions came from me. And your father let you believe this. But make no mistake, each decision about you children came from both of us.

And when your father disagreed with what I thought was best, he dug in and would not yield. He was a bit of a pain in the neck, your father, but he was my pain in the neck and I loved him.

So please know, my son, that the decision for you to work at the printshop came from both your father and me. We knew since you were born that we wanted more for you than working 14-hour days all your life at the boatyard and still living poor.

I never minded our poverty because I loved your father and loved you children and that made me feel like the richest woman in the world.

Yes, it was a dream of your father's that you would take over the business, Arthur. We both knew it was just a dream. A dream your father enjoyed and I let him have this pleasure.

All my nonsense of pretending our life was something different was just a dream. We all need to dream, my son, and I wanted to teach my children how to dream and not just accept the crumbs life throws at you.

Can I tell you one last silly thing? I have always had a bad heart, Arthur. The doctors all said that I should have died years ago. But I loved your father too much to leave him. Each time I saw his face, my heart would beat faster and I am convinced that is what kept me living so long. But he's gone now and I no longer see his face and I know this is why my heart is slowing down.

I'll say goodbye now, my lovely boy, and leave you with this last thought: when you put your head on your pillow tonight, remember your father's favorite saying: "Let go of the day's worries each night so there's room for tomorrow's joys."

I love you, Arthur,

May God bless you always, Mom

Arthur felt the weight of the world slide from his shoulders. *How could I have been so wrong about you, Mom? Please forgive me. I love you.*

And when he put his head on his pillow that night, he felt the burden of his sorrow leave. And for the first time in what felt like forever, he was hopeful for what joys tomorrow may bring.

"God bless you, Mom," he said in the darkness of his room.

❦·❦

"Such sorrow we cause ourselves," Arthur said aloud to George. "Such great and deep sorrow."

"Life can be cruel," said George.

"My parents were fine people. They truly and deeply loved the life they had together."

"A beautiful thing."

"They created a rich, wonderful world for themselves, shutting out all distractions around them. They cared for one another deeply and dedicated their lives to their family."

"A good way to live, Arthur."

"People today seem to need wealth and status before they think life is worthwhile. But for my parents, what they had was more than enough. As a matter of fact, it was everything. That's a rare quality, George, one I admire."

"I wonder why some people understand what is important in life and others don't."

"I couldn't say, George."

"It's a tough question, that's for sure. But I have a feeling if you figure out the answer, your dilemma will resolve itself."

"I have no idea what that means, George."

"I know you don't, Arthur, but I do. For now, that's enough."

CHAPTER 14
Emergency Council Meeting

Madge rushed Oscar when he returned from the market. "Oscar, Berris just told me Arthur is taking a day off. Can you believe it?"

"Good for him. If anyone deserves a day off, it's Arthur," he said, plopping down a heavy crate of fresh produce.

"No, Oscar, not good. Something is very wrong. We're closing The Café at 9 for an emergency council meeting. Hopefully, we can figure out what to do."

"What to do! Madge, really? If Arthur wants to take a day off, it's no one's business but his own. We are absolutely not closing to figure out what's bothering him. My advice to you and all the crazy people in this village is to mind your own business."

Just then, Caroline arrived. "Can I get some breakfast, Oscar? And who's closing The Café?" she added in eye-popping alarm.

"We're not closing," Oscar handed Caroline her usual to go. Black, no sugar.

Madge jumped in. "We are closing for an emergency council meeting this morning, Caroline. Arthur is taking a day off and no one knows why. He's just sitting up at his house on George doing nothing."

"That's bad, very bad," said Caroline. And with that, she picked up her coffee, walked to the door and said in a solemn voice, "I'll be back for the meeting."

Oscar shook his head at Caroline's dramatic departure.

"What about your breakfast?" he yelled after her. She yelled back, "Who can eat at a time like this?"

"Why is it that everyone in this village is bonkers?"

"That is absolutely not true and don't change the subject."

"Oh yeah, name me one sane person."

"Arthur. Arthur is as sane as they come."

"Now Madge, everyone likes Arthur, especially me. He's one of my closest friends. But he did name his bench George. And he has conversations with George, the bench...out loud. So, not completely sane in my book."

"Oh well, you have to be a little crazy to keep your sanity, don't you think? Besides, sane people are boring."

"You're a corker, Madge. But there's absolutely no way we are closing."

"Oscar, did you hear me correctly? You and I have both watched, from that very front window, Arthur cross-country ski down Main Street during a blizzard so he wouldn't miss work."

"I know that."

"And when the river rose and flooded the village, we also watched Arthur paddle his canoe by that front window so he wouldn't miss a day."

"I can see where you're going with this, Madge."

"Now, this same man, out of the blue, is taking a day off after 40 years. I can give more examples...."

Fully recognizing the look on Madge's face which said, *I'm digging in on this. Give it up*, Oscar threw in the towel. "I'll put more coffee on."

Just then, Constance walked in and couldn't resist a joke at Oscar's expense, "You'll need a lot of coffee, Oscar. Do you want me to run next door and put on some of my special brew?"

"You're bad," said Madge who couldn't resist a chuckle as she remembered *The Great Coffee Feud*.

CHAPTER 15
Getting Closer

A rthur's blood was boiling over like an unwatched pot. He was sick of thinking about the letter on the kitchen table. Sick of battling with George. And sick of trying to figure out why people think a day off was so great.

Yesterday was normal, he thought, pacing on the porch. *How is it possible in the span of 24 hours your life can be thrown into turmoil?*

He pointed a finger at George. "And don't you say a word."

"Mum's the word," said George.

However, George's reflection left Arthur in a contemplative mood. *If I figure out what is important in life, I'll solve my problem. What does that even mean?*

Arthur always felt he had a good grasp on what was important. He lived a modest life only spending money on the bare necessities. He indulged sparingly on trips to the theater and skipped vacations. Wealth and status meant nothing to him. He witnessed firsthand that neither brought peace nor happiness.

As far as love was concerned, it just wasn't in the cards. And at 62 years old, surely it was too late.

He had his memories and firmly believed in Tennyson's pearl of wisdom, *"Tis better to have loved and lost than never to have loved at all."*

"You're getting very good at rationalizing, Arthur. Something, I might point out, you're not known to do. A realistic approach is more your style."

"Oh, for heaven's sake, George, you're wearing me out. I'm not rationalizing."

"Seems like rationalizing to me."

"You're wrong." His voice was strained. "I'm being honest, sensible even."

"Honest! Arthur, stop kidding yourself. You're being a lot of things. Honest isn't one of them."

Arthur's pacing picked up speed. "You're asking me to make a decision that may change my life. A life, I might add, I'm perfectly happy with. It makes no sense. No sense at all."

"Do you hear yourself, Arthur?"

The simple question made Arthur realize how desperately he was avoiding the issue dominating his day. He sensed his justifications were not going to hold up much longer. He was shackled to his past. Admit it.

Arthur slumped low on the bench. *How will I resolve this mess?*

"When you open the damn letter!"

"Will you just shut up!"

CHAPTER 16
The Great Coffee Feud

The *Great Coffee Feud* raged five years earlier. It was mysterious to Oscar that he went through a dozen pots of coffee early morning but then hardly sold a cup after that.

"They go next door to the bookshop for the good stuff," Madge said distractedly as she wrote the daily specials on the board.

"What did you say? The good stuff. What is that?"

"Oscar, everyone in the village knows that Constance makes the best coffee on planet Earth. I suspect it's how she gets so many people to hang out at the shop."

"I never heard about this. And I categorically disagree that she has the best coffee. We serve a superior blend. I know it and you know it. Our coffee is the best."

"Nope," answered Madge. "Constance's coffee blows ours out of the water."

Oscar hunched and cleared his throat.

Madge cut him off. "And you haven't heard about this before because everyone in the village knew you would react exactly as you are carrying on now."

"And how is that?"

"Defensive and, I might add, a little crazy."

"My wife is a traitor," he mumbled as he flipped a pancake.

It missed the grill and plopped on the floor.

It was perfect timing, as they say, that Constance walked into The Café at that moment. Oscar was on her.

"Madge tells me she thinks your coffee is better than ours."

"It is," Constance simply stated and added in a playful voice, "by a mile."

"Well, answer me this, why does everyone in the village come to The Café first thing in the morning to get their coffee?"

"They come here first because I'm not open yet, Oscar. And, by the way, if I were open as early as you, they would come to The Page Turner first."

Voices were rising. Madge thought it prudent to jump in.

"Oscar, Constance has tasted your coffee plenty of times but you've never tasted hers. So why not go over for a cup? See what everyone is talking about."

"I don't have to, Madge. I already know my coffee is the best!" He waved his arm like a bandleader.

Constance threw the gauntlet down. "Sounds like you're chicken?"

Conversation in The Café came to a grinding halt. All eyes fixed on Oscar.

He never backed down from a challenge. His eyes blazed. His shoulders squared. "I will be there at 3 pm and we'll see whose coffee is best!"

Well, word of *The Great Coffee Feud* spread throughout

Stones End like a house on fire. Shopkeepers started drawing up signs: *Gone to The Great Coffee Feud. Be back when it's over.*

Berris burst through the door of the bakery. "Oscar just found out about Constance's coffee."

"Oh boy. Does he know that's where the whole village goes?" said Mrs. Kruchinski.

"Yes, indeedy, and he's not happy, Mrs. K. Not happy at all."

"Was that little vein on his neck showing?"

"Positively bulging."

"And wait till you hear the rest. He's going to the bookshop at 3 for a taste."

Mrs. Kruchinski clapped her hands together loudly. "I wouldn't miss this for the world. You going?"

"Is the Pope Catholic?"

Coffee was the lifeblood to the residents of Stones End. The elixir of life. The nectar of the gods. No thought took hold until that first morning sip burned their taste buds and pulsed through their bodies.

No one would miss *The Great Coffee Feud.*

The excited villagers started for the bookshop at 2 pm to get a good seat. Within a half-hour, it was SRO.

Martin was jammed up against the front window watching for Oscar. At 2:59, he yelled, "He's coming."

The room went silent.

Oscar marched through the door. Madge, looking completely amused, was close behind him. He solemnly walked to the counter where Constance was waiting.

"Well," he said, "let's get this over with." A stone-faced Constance handed him a fresh cup.

He lifted the cup and took a long, deep sniff. Villagers murmured. Oscar's eyebrows lifted slightly. The tension was mounting. You'd need a hatchet to cut the air.

Then Oscar put the cup to his mouth and the room went deathly still. This time Oscar's eyebrows shot straight up. Whispered speculation ran wild. "He knows!"

Oscar took another sip and another until he finished the whole cup. The coffee was so bloody good, he wanted to lick the cup clean. Then he fixed his stare at Constance who returned a flinty one of her own. The tension was unbearable.

Madge couldn't stand it any longer. "Well, what do you think?"

And Oscar replied, "What the hell do you put in it that makes it so bloody good?"

The crowd went wild as every villager thought, *we no longer have to sneak past The Café when Oscar's back is turned. He knows. He finally knows!*

No one expected Constance's reply. It still rankles Oscar to this day. Using her most innocent voice, she said, "Sorry, Oscar, but it's a secret family recipe. No sharing."

You'd think someone knocked him in the back of the head with a 2X4. "Oh no you don't. You have to share the ingredients. I would share with you."

"What part of *secret* aren't you getting?"

And that started the friendly, but edgy, coffee feud between Oscar and Constance.

CHAPTER 17
Rounding Up the Troops

Mrs. Kruchinski marched into The Café promptly at 9 am like a general entering a war room.

Oscar rolled his eyes at the dramatic entrance. He was already feeling tormented.

"Olga, is it true that Arthur isn't at work? I just can't believe it. I don't remember Arthur ever taking a day off," said Constance. She had noticed a change in Arthur recently and was secretly worried. And now this!

"It's true and you don't remember because it's a first. I saw him with my own eyes sitting on that bench of his, not getting ready for work, not doing anything. Just sitting."

"Really, just sitting there. So unlike Arthur. I've never seen Arthur sitting still during the day. He's always moving."

The door to The Café opened again and in walked Berris, Martin and Birdie.

Birdie's mouth set in a hard line at the sight of Mrs. Kruchinski. She pulled Madge over to the side and said, "It's for Arthur. So, I'm here. Just keep that woman away from me. Where is everyone? We need to get started."

Birdie and Mrs. Kruchinski stayed clear of each other, by 50 feet, more if possible. The Incident was a raw spot in the village. They knew to stay out of the crossfire.

Berris observed to Madge: "Is it a good idea for Birdie and

Mrs. K to be here together? We're not going to witness World War III, are we?"

"Let's hope for the best," said Madge. A deep crease marked her forehead.

"Why can't people be on time?" said Mrs. Kruchinski. "They know how urgent this is. Five more minutes. That's all."

"Oh, for heaven's sake, Olga. This is not an emergency," said Oscar.

"Really. You don't think we should worry about Arthur skipping work?" Mrs. Kruchinski asked thrusting her face toward Oscar.

Oscar choked down the impulse to give her a good whack. He bit his tongue and disappeared behind the counter.

A tick above Madge's eye started jumping. Oscar was already agitated. Berris was upset. Constance was worried. And Birdie was pissed. *Let's hope we can get through this meeting alive.*

CHAPTER 18
The Decision

I envy you your happiness, little one. You don't have a mysterious letter sitting in your nest back home, do you? Of course, you don't. I bet you were smarter than I was and kept your heart to yourself.

The tiny sparrow just hopped around in a rhythmic dance.

Arthur went into the house for more coffee and heard George call after him: "You're not going to have a fourth cup, are you? You'll get the jitters."

"I am going to have a fourth cup, George, and I never get the jitters," Arthur yelled back.

He pushed the button and waited for the strong, dark liquid to drip.

The robust aroma filled the kitchen and Arthur instinctively reached for his cup.

As he turned to leave, his eyes fell on the letter. His instincts told him to keep walking but he stood frozen in place.

Arthur stared at the letter willing it to give up its secrets. For a moment he was sure it was staring back.

Without warning, it started taunting him. Repeated chants pounded back and forth: *Open me, keep it hidden.* They wouldn't stop.

A cold shiver shot down his spine. *It's taking on a life of its own.*

Arthur's head was reeling as the silent pleas raged on. He covered his ears and closed his eyes tightly trying to stop the battle.

"What do you want from me?" he cried out.

His shout silenced the voices. Arthur's heart was racing. His palms were sweaty. Desperately, he needed to be someplace else...now!

Suddenly, he was on the cliff high above the Mediterranean Sea with her. He could feel their first kiss as if it were yesterday. She was entwined in his arms again. The promise of the wonderful life before them filled his heart. It was all so real, he was sure she was by his side.

Arthur opened his eyes. The peaceful memory calmed him. He leaned against the counter to steady himself and taking a large mouthful of coffee, an unexpected thought slowly drifted by...*sometimes the gods favor you with a second chance.*

Could the answer be so simple?

Arthur reached for the letter. His hand trembled slightly. He could feel sweat break out on his brow.

This is it. The hope of love's second chance? Or the certainty of love's memory?

Time came to a halt as he faced off against the agonizing decision. The moments dragged as though eternity found a home.

Suddenly, a cloud blocked the sun robbing the kitchen of its comforting light. Arthur blinked to adjust. And with this small shift of light, his hopeful heart drained.

For in that one tiny moment, when light changed to shadow, the letter revealed its truth. Arthur clutched the sad remnant of a once-beautiful rose left unattended far too long.

A long sigh marked his decision. *It was a lifetime ago. Another world.*

Arthur tenderly placed the letter on the table, walked out to the porch and announced to George, "I've made my decision. I'm not opening the letter."

"No, Arthur. No. You're making the wrong decision."

"It's done. And I'll live with the right or wrong of it," Arthur said. He flexed his fingers like a boxer. "Time to move on."

"Arthur, you're choosing to live in the shadow of your memories. You could be walking toward a bright future that may hold the possibility of love."

"I'm too old, George." Arthur clenched his fists. "There's nothing wrong with my life as it is. I cherish my memories and I won't let a chance of love trespass on them."

"You can't hold a memory in your arms."

"Very poetic, George. But my memories have been a constant source of comfort for 40 years. Besides, I've always been fine living in the shadows."

"You deserve more, Arthur. Living in the shadows always casts a dim view on life. You're a good man and you deserve more. Why are you choosing to shortchange yourself? Turn around, Arthur. Turn around and face the sun."

"That's enough. My decision is final."

I'm running out of ammunition, thought George frantically. *I hope the cavalry arrives soon.*

CHAPTER 19
The Incident

Birdie sat as far away from Mrs. Kruchinski as possible. As she took her seat, her eyes locked with Madge's and both women knew they were thinking of *The Incident....*

It was a beautiful autumn day when the little white dog showed up in the village. The morning air was scented with the musty smell of wet leaves and an unseasonable chilly wind caused villagers to put up their collars and quicken their steps.

Now of all the places in Stones End the stray dog could have rested, he made the grave mistake of parking himself in front of the bakery.

Mrs. Kruchinski tried for the better part of the morning to shoo her unwelcome tenant away. She finally called the sheriff's office.

"I have a stray dog sitting out front," she told Caroline, the deputy.

"So, what do you want the sheriff's office to do about it?"

"Come and take it to the pound!" she bellowed.

"Yes, I'll get on that right away." Caroline had no intention of doing any such thing since she believed the pound was entirely unsuitable for God's noblest creatures.

All morning long, the door to The Café steadily swung open with villagers inquiring about the dog.

TURNING TOWARD THE SUN

When Constance caught sight of him, she immediately ran next door.

"Has anyone seen this dog before?" she asked Madge.

"Never. And can you believe he parked himself right in front of the bakery? I took him some food and water earlier and Olga almost chewed my head off."

"Let me guess," said Walter. "Filthy beasts, dogs are. They track dirt everywhere, shed fur all over the place and they drool!"

"Sounds like Olga, alright," Oscar laughed.

"No. She pretty much said, 'Don't feed him. He'll never leave.'"

"Well, I agree. The poor thing picked the wrong spot to hang out," said Constance.

No one could resist petting the new furry villager but the dog didn't give up so much as a tail wag. Concern for whether he was sick prompted talk about taking him over to Doc Johnson, the vet.

"He looks OK to me," said Oscar. "Maybe he's just shy."

"I don't know about that," said Walter. "A dog that doesn't respond to a good scratch behind the ears doesn't seem normal to me. I think he's sick."

Then a wondrous thing happened. At the first sight of Birdie turning onto Main Street, the little white dog jerked his head in her direction and ran straight for her.

"Would you look at that," Madge said with delight. "He

loves Birdie."

"Well, what do you know? Doesn't pay attention to anyone all morning and then Birdie comes along and bam," said Oscar. "Wonders never cease."

Birdie was overjoyed with the affection of her new best friend. It was love at first sight for both of them. She named him after her favorite thing in the whole world: Brownie.

Old Horace, the mail carrier, made the mistake of questioning Birdie's choice. "You named a white dog Brownie. Why not Snowball or Marshmallow?"

"Because I hate marshmallows and abhor snowballs." Birdie replied with a wild wave of her arm. "One would think that was obvious."

Well, it wasn't obvious to Horace. Birdie's logic always escaped him. So, he did the wise thing and walked away.

Birdie and Brownie were inseparable from that moment on. They even attended Sunday Mass together.

Now the problem started the very first time Birdie brought Brownie into The Café. Mrs. Kruchinski came in for her usual tuna salad sandwich for lunch and noticed Brownie at a table with Birdie.

"Dogs don't belong in food establishments," she complained to Madge. "It's against the health code."

Madge tried to calm her. "He's not bothering anyone, Olga. No one seems to mind." But Mrs. Kruchinski stomped out.

From that day forward, she threw a fit every time she saw

Brownie in The Café. She stopped complaining to Madge and took her complaints to Oscar instead. And when Oscar didn't heed her warnings, she threatened to take it to the Board of Health.

"Olga is going to cause trouble over this," Madge said to Oscar.

"She'll calm down, eventually."

"I warned them," Mrs. Kruchinski told Karl, her husband.

Karl was a burly man. Double X in size but all muscle. He owned a landscaping and pool business in the county. Physically demanding jobs that kept him in shape. Most considered him honest, dependable and levelheaded. No one ever had a bad word to say about Karl.

"Olga, how many times have I told you? These people are not only our clients, but they are also our neighbors, our friends. We have to live in this village. Don't cause trouble."

"I'm not the one causing trouble."

"For heaven's sake, Olga. That dog is the best thing that ever happened to old Birdie. I've never seen her so happy. Would it kill you to just ignore him?"

"Yes, Karl, it would kill me. Dogs do not belong in restaurants. And can you believe there was dog hair in my sandwich the other day?"

Karl threw up his hands and walked away.

Against Karl's warning, Mrs. Kruchinski called the health squad.

And then, as they say, all hell broke loose.

The Café received a summons. Oscar was furious. So, when Mrs. Kruchinski came in, words got ugly.

"Olga! Were you the one who sicced the health police on me?"

"I did indeed. I warned you and I warned Madge. That dog does not belong in a food establishment."

"The Café received a summons!"

"And whose fault is that? If you had just removed the dog like I told you, you wouldn't have...."

He interrupted. "Well, how about this, Olga? I'll remove you from The Café and Brownie gets to stay."

And then the unthinkable happened.

Without warning, Brownie broke loose, charged across the floor and bit Mrs. Kruchinski's leg.

"He bit me. He bit me," she screamed. Blood was gushing down her leg and pooling on the floor.

"Oh my God, she's bleeding," screamed Constance.

Horace tripped over his mail sack trying to get to Mrs. Kruchinski.

Walter dropped his burger as he sprung off the counter stool.

Birdie panicked. She grabbed Brownie and made a run for it.

Diners huddled wanting to do something but were mostly in the way.

Madge and Oscar knew this was trouble with a capital T.

"Olga, sit down and let us clean the wound."

Mrs. Kruchinski refused help and hobbled out the door. "You haven't heard the last of this."

An eerie quiet shrouded the village waiting for Mrs. Kruchinski's retribution which they were certain would be swift.

Birdie hid in her house too afraid to take Brownie out for his afternoon walk. Madge and Oscar couldn't work, couldn't focus and could barely talk waiting for the health police to shut them down.

Constance jumped into action.

As soon as Mrs. Kruchinski ran out, Constance scooted next door and called Karl. *If there was anyone who could calm Olga down, it was Karl,* she thought.

Karl, bless his soul, came running to Olga's aid. But after he tended her wounds, he read her the riot act. "Olga, you do anything to have that dog taken away from poor old Birdie or anything to get The Café shut down and you'll have my anger to deal with. Do you understand?"

Mrs. Kruchinski stepped back from Karl's anger. She did not utter a single word. *You have to pick your battles,* she thought but deep down regretted taking things too far.

So, she showed up in the village the next day as though nothing had happened. She never spoke of it again.

Oscar told Birdie to tie up Brownie outside when she came in. Birdie could barely eat as Brownie yelped.

Mrs. Kruchinski ate at The Café every day. Birdie never

again entered the bakery. And no one in Stones End ever spoke of *The Incident* again.

Rounding Up the Troops - Continued

"Is this it?" asked Mrs. Kruchinski. "We still need Father Gregory and Caroline. I called my Karl, but he's in the middle of a pool installation. He'll get here if he can but I am to keep him informed via text."

"You text?" asked a shocked Berris.

"Yes, Berris, I text. I'm a modern woman, don't you know."

"Well, shut me up," said Berris.

"I agree, Olga. Father Gregory should be here. I'll call the rectory," said Madge.

"Their phone is not working. I just saw the repair truck," said Martin. "I'll dash up and get him."

"For heaven's sake. People are going and no one is coming. We'll never get started. And Caroline, we need Caroline," shouted Mrs. Kruchinski.

CHAPTER 20
Caroline, Internet Surfer Extraordinaire

C aroline's mind was spinning like a dog chasing his tail. *What could possibly be wrong with Arthur? Nothing is ever wrong with him. This is big! I wonder if he's sick. Oh God, don't even go there. Maybe a family member is sick. Come to think of it, does he even have family?* Her investigative mind was considering all possibilities.

Caroline, the deputy sheriff for Stones End, was a no-nonsense officer of the law. Always on duty, it seemed. She was deadly serious about her job and carried herself in an official capacity at all times right down to never being seen out of uniform.

She was in her early thirties, with stick-straight hair which she tied in a severe bun and was known for her brusque manner. Just the facts, ma'am.

Despite her rough edges, the villagers relied on her fairness and levelheaded approach to keep Stones End in order. Overall, she was a well-liked and respected member of the close-knit community.

Now, Caroline did have one off-putting quality. She had a peculiar proclivity for seeing dastardly, evil plots in the most innocent of circumstances. Like when Mrs. McCarthy left her philandering, no-good cheat of a husband. Caroline was sure Mr. McCarthy murdered her.

She was told time and again that Mrs. McCarthy went to live with her sister in New York but it took Caroline a full month before she closed the investigation.

"It's from all those murder mysteries she reads," said Mrs. Kruchinski. "Makes your mind go goofy."

But aside from this small quirk, Caroline had a brilliant investigative mind. She could solve any problem, puzzle or mystery presented and was the best internet surfer the village had ever seen.

They would spend weeks hopelessly looking for a piece of information on the web and finally throw in the towel and call Caroline.

Caroline would walk in, sit at the computer and within minutes would ask, "Is this what you're looking for?" And it was always exactly what they were looking for.

Heads would wag back and forth in awe. "How does she do that?"

"It's a gift," Caroline would reply with a shrug.

Rounding Up the Troops - Continued

"Where's Walter?" Madge asked. "He said he would be at the meeting. He may be a good source of information. You know a barbershop is a hotbed of gossip. While all that haircutting is going on, he might have overheard something."

Constance laughed at the image this conjured but Birdie jumped up and said, "Excellent idea. I'll run and get him."

"He knows about the meeting," Madge yelled after Birdie, but she was already out the door.

"Another one going," said Mrs. Kruchinski impatiently.

CHAPTER 21
Walter, Resident Virtuoso

W alter owned the barbershop next to The Café and was known to love opera almost as much as his mother's lasagna. He was sure his Italian heritage spurred his passion. "It's in my blood," he was often heard to say.

He was a distinguished gentleman sporting a full head of salt-and-pepper hair, blazing blue eyes and a complexion that always looked bronzed.

His mother often told him he had classic Roman features but Walter knew that just meant he had a big nose, which he secretly hated. He wasn't a tall man, maybe 5 foot 9, without an ounce of body fat. And the ease with which he moved made him appear much younger than his 60 years.

He spoke with a slight Italian accent which the women in the village considered wonderfully romantic. "I could listen to Walter all day long," Berris would say dreamily.

He named his shop, The Barber of Stones End which was meant as a clever play on "The Barber of Seville." Unfortunately, the whimsical nuance was lost to most villagers who just thought it was a weird name.

They didn't share his Italian passion. But Walter had enough for them all. His shop was a slice of Italy: "Tosca," "Rigoletto" and "La Traviata" mingled with potted fig trees, cannolis and, of course, espresso.

Walter had a rich tenor voice and a secret desire to sing in a major opera production. Villagers encouraged him constantly to audition at The Met. "And who would cut your hair?" Walter would reply jovially.

Now Walter never shared the fact that he did actually audition at The Met as a boy. His mother arranged it when he was 10. Walter was both terrified and excited at the prospect. He practiced night and day.

The near-zero temperature was biting. His mother worried about how the cold air would affect Walter's voice as they headed to the audition. But she never wavered in her certainty that they would accept him on the spot.

Walter felt dwarfed on the oaken stage that bore his opera heroes through the centuries. His knees could buckle any moment ending his career without uttering a stanza.

His thoughts and nerves ran wild. *What if I open my mouth and nothing comes out? Or worse, I make a hideous croaking sound? Or worse still, I forget the lyrics?*

The intro music started and the first note escaping from Walter's mouth was horribly out of key. His mother winced.

But then the music entered his soul as it always did and carried him to that glorious place where only opera music lived. And from there, Walter's performance was not only perfect, it was stunning.

The final note rocketed him to the roof of The Met. He delivered his absolute best performance which he desperately hoped made up for his botched first note.

He looked to the left of the massive stage and saw his mother dabbing her eyes with her handkerchief and enthusiastically throwing a thumbs-up.

I've got this! he thought.

His euphoric state came to an abrupt halt. The dreaded words hit his ears like a hard slap. "Thank you. We'll be in touch."

But as Walter would quickly find out, those words would not be the worst part of his day. His mother stepped from the wings and challenged the panel of judges.

"I happen to have an excellent ear for music and perfect pitch. I know my son made a mistake on the first note, but his performance was the best of the day. And you all know it."

One of the judges slowly pulled off his glasses, looked at Walter's mother as though she was a bothersome insect. "My dear woman, there are two elements to every performance: voice and nerves. A performer must have complete control of each. We'll be in touch!" he snapped.

Walter was mortified and dragged his mother from the stage.

Always the optimist, she assured Walter, "They'll come to their senses, dear, you'll see. We'll just have to wait."

Walter knew it was over. He would never hear from The Met. It took his mother till June to accept defeat.

That summer, Walter lived in a funk and hardly left his room. He kept reliving the one botched note as well as the humiliation of his mother's words. And the worst part of the whole summer was that he no longer wanted to sing.

His mother tried everything to get Walter to snap out of his depression. She loaded "Pagliacci," his favorite opera, on the record player and waited to hear Walter join in as he always did. No sound came from his room.

And then an unexpected solution presented itself. Upon seeing "Les Misérables," Walter's Aunt Gina rushed to tell his mother about the remarkable experience.

"Theresa, the music was so powerful, so moving, it just took my breath away. And I kept thinking Walter would absolutely love it."

So, as an end-of-summer treat, Walter's mother took him to see "Les Misérables." That did the trick. Upon returning home, Walter immediately played the soundtrack his mother bought him. He started singing again and never stopped.

But no matter how many times his mother pleaded with him to audition again at The Met, Walter refused.

"Mama, I know I have a good voice. It's just not good enough for The Met. Please, just let it go."

Walter's mother didn't agree but for Walter's sake, she sadly released the hold of her dream. And as Walter grew to be a man, he cheerfully accepted his lot in life. He would follow in his father's footsteps and cut hair for a living.

His experience of standing on stage at The Met and looking out onto that glorious opera house, however, left him with an unquenchable desire to perform. So, Walter delighted the residents of Stones End with opera concerts.

He performed the first Friday of each month in front of the barbershop. Enthusiasm for the concert was intoxicating, contagious. The night was more than great music. It was hanging out with dear friends, the chance to make new friends. Trying new foods, tasting new wines. Sharing news, spreading gossip. The village was alive with comforting scents, familiar faces and rousing conversations.

Shop doors slammed shut promptly at 5 pm to prepare. Concertgoers jockeyed early to anchor their lawn chairs. Shopkeepers stretched strands of white lights from their awnings. Karl and Horace turned up the sound system.

Mrs. Kruchinski adorned an elegant table on the sidewalk in front of the bakery with linen and candelabra and overflowing with loaves of bread and pastries.

The wine shop did likewise, setting out a wine-tasting table. Oscar, not one to be outdone, offered a smorgasbord of tantalizing hors d'oeurvres.

Karl, who grew up in Vienna, especially loved the concerts. It stirred warm memories of attending the opera with his parents as a boy.

There was a Lighting of the Candles ceremony to mark the start of every concert. And so, when the sun went down, one by one, the candles on the sidewalk tables were lit and the street looked like an outdoor cathedral.

Next, the strands of white lights were switched on. The magical lights twinkled. Oohs and aahs erupted. It never got old.

And finally, the concert began. Villagers sat under a starlit sky while Walter's remarkable voice took them to Egypt, Spain, France. They ate and sang, and laughed and drank and never went home disappointed.

CHAPTER 22
Start of the Council Meeting

"Hallelujah," said Mrs. Kruchinski, throwing her hands high in the air as the missing members arrived.

"We're all here. Let's begin," said Oscar. His foot was rapidly tapping the floor.

Caroline took the lead and, to everyone's surprise, Mrs. Kruchinski let her.

"Now, I think we should start by going around the table and each tells if they've recently noticed anything different about Arthur's behavior."

Heads nodded. This was the most logical approach.

Walter, at the head of the table, started.

"As we all know, Arthur comes in once a month like clockwork for a cut. And then just like that, no Arthur last week. It was a topic of discussion among the regulars, I can tell you."

This news raised eyebrows around the table. Arthur was never late getting a trim.

"Did anything happen the last time Arthur was in?" asked Caroline.

"No, no, I can't say there was. Wait a minute, something did happen." Bodies shifted closer.

"When Arthur was paying for his cut, he was talking about

something, I don't remember what it was. All of a sudden, he stopped in mid-sentence and just stood there staring at the wall behind the register."

"What on Earth was he looking at?" asked Madge.

"He noticed the opera poster I hung there that morning. I have to tell you, it clearly upset him. The color drained out of his face. He stared at it and then without saying a word, turned and walked out of the shop."

"We need that poster!" shouted Mrs. Kruchinski. "It may be the key to what is upsetting Arthur."

"I'm on it," said Walter and was out the door in a flash. "Don't say anything important until I return."

"An opera poster upsetting Arthur," said Constance. "How mysterious."

And then Martin dropped the first bombshell. "Well, I have something significant to add." They all sat at attention.

"Every once in a while, we get a rush job. This causes me to be late with the daily report which I always have ready for Arthur before he leaves for the day."

Now Martin was known to be long-winded in his stories, so Oscar interrupted. "Let's zip along smartly, Martin. Meeting or no meeting, the door to The Café opens sharply at 10." Madge shot him a look. Oscar shot her one back holding his ground.

"Yes, yes, indeed," said Martin. "Well now, where was I? Oh yes, two weeks ago, I stayed late to finish the report, then took it to Arthur's home. When I got there, Arthur was in his workshop, as usual. You know how he just loves his woodworking."

"Tick tock, tick tock," Oscar said. "And stop shooting daggers at me, Madge."

"Yes, yes, I'm digressing, please forgive me. Now, where was I? Oh yes, Arthur told me to leave the report on the table inside. I don't know why, but I walked right by the hall table and brought the report into the kitchen and put it on that table. And you'll never guess what I saw?"

Here Martin paused for effect. Oscar repeated, "Tick tock, tick tock," but others yelled, "What did you find?"

"Well," said Martin, "on the kitchen table was a letter. And you'll never guess where it's from?"

"Oh, for heaven's sake, Martin, spit it out," said Birdie slamming her hand down.

"The Metropolitan Opera House in New York City!"

Audible gasps made tense air thicker. Caroline jumped up from her chair and said, "I'm getting a very bad feeling."

Walter came running back with the poster in hand just as the gasps echoed. "Oh my gosh. What did I miss?"

Mrs. Kruchinski filled Walter in. He, too, gasped.

And then Martin announced in an overly dramatic voice, "There's more!"

Now even Oscar was intrigued. He moved to the edge of his chair. "Go on, Martin."

"Last week we had another rush job causing me to take the late daily report to Arthur's house. I made it a point of putting the report on the kitchen table so I could see if the mystery letter was still there. And guess what I saw?"

Oscar shot him a look.

"Yes, yes, sorry. The letter was still there and in the same exact spot as though it hadn't been touched. So, I took the liberty of picking it up and you won't believe it when I tell you." This time they all shot Martin a look.

"The letter had not been opened!"

"Oh my God, he killed her. He killed the opera star and has been hiding in this village ever since and now someone has finally caught up with him," Caroline blurted out.

"Oh, for heaven's sake, Caroline, Arthur is not a murderer!" said Father Gregory. "Get hold of yourself, please."

The room went quiet as a church as everyone pondered this development. It was Birdie who interrupted.

"It's obvious, isn't it? We won't know how to proceed without knowing the contents of that letter."

"I agree. Who leaves an unopened letter laying around for two weeks unless they're fearful of what it says?" said Walter.

"Exactly. Something catastrophic happened in Arthur's past. Something he prefers to forget. And this letter threatens to open Pandora's Box."

They were all astounded at Birdie's insight but knew it was a plausible theory.

Mrs. Kruchinski proposed the next step.

"Well, my friends, it doesn't appear that Arthur is going to open the letter on his own which, of course, means one of us has to go to his house and get him to open it."

All eyes slowly turned and fixed on Father Gregory.

"No, you can throw that right out of your heads. You know how I hate prying. It's a gross invasion of privacy. I won't do it!" He folded his arms across his chest like a petulant child.

"Now you listen to me, Gregory. You're one of Arthur's closest friends," said Birdie. "And a priest. So, you know how to handle delicate situations."

"I don't like where you're going with this," said Father Gregory. His voice was quivering.

"Never mind that. If you don't do it, one of us has to. And just look around this table, do any of us look like we know what we're doing?"

There were more than a few humphs as a reaction to Birdie's comment but then eyes slowly refocused on Father Gregory.

Birdie has a point. Father Gregory pondered poor Arthur under Mrs. Kruchinski's interrogation.

"Fine. I'll go. But I want it on record that I'm not happy about this!"

"Yes, yes. It's on record. Now, go!" said Mrs. Kruchinski.

"We'll stay here and study the poster," Caroline called after him.

Father Gregory slowly plodded toward Arthur's home.

CHAPTER 23
Father Gregory, The Spy

"Oh, who is this now?" said Arthur at the sound of more footsteps on the path. When Father Gregory rounded the corner, Arthur fell back in laughter. "I was hoping it would be you they sent."

"You knew they would send someone?"

"Of course. I know this village well. Olga saw me sitting on George this morning then ran into the village and sounded the alarm."

"She did, indeed."

"Then I made the mortal mistake of telling Martin that I was taking a day off and that sealed my fate. Let me guess, an emergency council meeting?"

Father Gregory doubled over holding his side.

"You do know this village well. But you, my friend, have caused quite a beehive of activity this morning. So, yes, an emergency council meeting," he said taking a seat next to Arthur.

"See...they can't fool me."

"Well, then I'm sure you know I've been sent on a fact-finding mission."

"They're good, Gregory, but I believe they will be stumped this time."

"I'm not so sure about that, Arthur. Martin was there."

"Uh oh, he's trouble." His brows knit tightly together. "He notices everything. But, no, not even Martin will figure this one out."

"And Caroline too."

"She's double trouble," Arthur said tapping the side of the bench. But then he shook his head confidently saying, "No, trust me, Gregory, this will even stump the two super sleuths."

"They already know about the letter, Arthur."

His pulse started thumping.

Father Gregory blurted out rapidly like a newscaster. "Martin saw it on your kitchen table twice over the past two weeks and that the letter was from The Metropolitan Opera."

"That kid can be a menace."

"The second time he saw the letter, it was still unopened."

"And damn nosy." His face twisted in a scowl.

"And Walter remembered that you reacted strangely to a new opera poster he put up in the barbershop. And everyone is concerned that you are one week late in getting your haircut."

An open-mouthed Arthur looked at Father Gregory. "They're good. They're very good, Gregory. I'll give them that. But they won't have guessed what's in the letter because I haven't opened it."

Arthur's mood suddenly changed to anger at the thought of anyone knowing the dark chapter in his past. "It's none of their damn business, Gregory." Then added, "Sorry for swearing."

"No worries, Arthur. I might have said worse if I were in your shoes. But something is bothering you, my friend, and has been for a while."

"Has it been that noticeable?"

"Very. They say sharing a burden lightens the load. And it will eventually be discovered. The super sleuths, as you call them, are researching the opera poster and the opera star as we speak."

The walls are closing in on me, Arthur thought.

Dealing with the letter was exhausting him as much as arguing with George.

Feeling defeated, Arthur said, "Alright, Gregory, I'll tell you what's going on. It's a painful chapter of my life and one that I have never shared with another living soul."

Father Gregory sat down next to Arthur and braced himself as he already felt the pain emanating from his dear friend.

CHAPTER 24
Do We Know Arthur Covington at All?

"Walter, let's see this mysterious poster that sent Arthur into a tizzy," said Mrs. Kruchinski.

"Righto," said Walter. He placed the opera poster on the table.

"What are we looking at?" asked Berris.

"A poster of one of the greatest operas of all time. It's called 'La Boehme' and was composed by the great Giacomo Puccini."

"Never heard of it," said Oscar, rapidly tapping his pencil as the meeting dragged on.

"The poster is announcing Ana Felicia's swan song. She's a world-renowned opera singer and this will be her final performance."

"So, what could Arthur's connection be to this opera?" asked Berris.

"Maybe it's not the opera he has a connection to. Maybe it's the opera singer," said Martin. "After all, he did get a letter from a woman with a return address of The Met."

"How do you know the letter is from a woman?" asked Constance.

"Flowery handwriting. Had to be a woman."

"Yes, yes," said Caroline. "Very good, Martin."

"That's crazy," said Mrs. Kruchinski. "How on Earth would Arthur know a famous opera star? Where is she from, anyway?"

"Madrid, she grew up in Madrid," said Walter. He followed Ana Felicia's career from the start.

"There you go," said Mrs. Kruchinski. "Arthur grew up in England. So how would he know someone in Spain, not to mention, a famous opera singer?"

Then it was Constance's turn to drop a bombshell. "Arthur didn't grow up in England, Olga. He was born in Greece."

The news was met with stunned silence.

"Greece!" shouted Mrs. Kruchinski. "Arthur's not Greek, he's English. His name is Arthur Covington. Does that sound Greek to you?"

She went on with her version of Arthur's life history in her usual know-it-all fashion.

"Arthur was born in England and was an only child who lived at home with his parents until they died. He then came to America to work with his uncle, his only living relative, at the printshop. So, he's lived in England and America. No Greece."

"No, Olga," Constance said. "You're wrong."

Berris closed her eyes and held her breath waiting for the fireworks. Mrs. Kruchinski was never wrong.

But Constance was determined to set the record straight. Even though she was not one to share anything she knew about Arthur, she felt he was in trouble.

"Arthur's father was British but his mother was Greek. His father met his mother when he spent a summer in Greece. He visited with one of his uncles who bought a boatyard there years before."

"I never heard this," said Mrs. Kruchinski. She waved a dismissive hand.

"Pay her no attention, Constance," said Oscar. He narrowed his eyes toward the mistaken know-it-all.

"During that summer, Arthur's father and mother fell madly in love and married. His father went to work for his uncle. When his uncle died, he left the boatyard to Arthur's father."

Mrs. Kruchinski's mouth was hanging open.

Constance added that Arthur was not an only child. He was the youngest of four Covington children and he had a brother and two sisters.

Mrs. Kruchinski couldn't stand it any longer and challenged Constance. "It makes no sense what you're saying. How do you know all of this?"

"Right from the horse's mouth," Constance said defiantly. "Arthur told me."

"And siblings, he told you about siblings?"

"Yes, he did. I've even seen letters from them."

"Ah-ha," shouted Mrs. Kruchinski abruptly rising and knocking her chair over. "Impossible! If Arthur received letters from siblings abroad, everyone in the village would know about it!"

All agreed. Evelyn, who ran the post office, was a blabber-mouth. If Arthur received letters from abroad, not to mention one from the Metropolitan Opera House in New York, news would be all over the village.

Then Martin quietly interjected, "Arthur has a secret post office box in the city. I suspect that's where he receives the letters from his siblings and where he picked up the mystery letter."

The tension felt as heavy as a London fog. Walter was shaking his head trying to clear his confusion. Birdie sat with her hand under her chin looking like Rodin's "The Thinker." Oscar and Madge just sat hang-jawed.

A secret post office box. *What could he be hiding?* The question hovered like a foreboding cloud above them.

"Well, Birdie, I believe you're right. Pandora's Box has definitely been opened," said Caroline. She then launched into a summary of events that sounded more like a police report.

"Let's recap everyone, shall we?"

1. Arthur goes pale upon looking at a poster of an upcoming opera where a famous opera star is giving her final performance at the Metropolitan Opera House in New York City. Puzzling.

2. Arthur is one week late for his haircut possibly not wanting to enter the barbershop where he might see the aforementioned poster. Worrisome.

3. Arthur, who has never missed a day of work in his life, suddenly takes a day off. Unbelievable.

4. Arthur lies to Mrs. Kruchinski and Martin about the reason for the day off saying it's because he is tired when, clearly, the unopened letter is getting to him. Unfathomable.

5. Arthur was born in Greece, not England. Shocking.

6. Arthur is not an only child but has three siblings. Surprising.

7. Arthur receives a letter from a famous opera star...unopened for at least two weeks. Mysterious.

8. Arthur, who has a mailbox in the village, keeps a secret post office box in the city. Doubly mysterious.

"Have I missed anything?"

No one could answer. They all sat in uncharacteristic silence. It certainly appeared that Arthur was hiding something.

Finally, Caroline said aloud the question on everyone's mind, "My friends, do we know Arthur Covington at all?"

The ominous question hung heavy in the air. No one knew what to think or even how to continue. It was Caroline who abruptly snapped everyone back to attention.

"Back to the poster. Let's stay focused and start with Arthur's possible connection with this opera singer. What's her name?"

"Ana Felicia," said Walter. "I don't see how there can be a connection. Ana Felicia grew up in Madrid and Arthur grew up in Greece."

Deputy Caroline opened her laptop, cracked her knuckles, gave a long stretch of her neck and went to work. After a few short moments, she triumphantly shouted, "Got it! Ana Felicia did not grow up in Spain. She grew up in Greece!"

Mrs. Kruchinski almost fainted.

"There's our connection. My guess is that Arthur had an affair with Ana Felicia. It ended badly. Maybe an unwanted child was involved. Now, years later, she's contacting him out of the blue for God only knows what reason. That's it, that's it, I'm certain!"

"Well, that's it," said Mrs. Kruchinski. "We're on hold until Father Gregory returns with news. Let's all pray that he gets Arthur to open that blasted letter!"

"Finally," said Oscar as he let in the waiting customers.

Berris said, "Yep, I gotta open too. Gracie will be waiting. I'm doing hi-lites in her hair."

"Me too," said Birdie. "Time to walk Brownie."

Walter left singing from "La Boehme."

And no one but Martin noticed that Constance left without saying a word holding back tears.

CHAPTER 25
Constance, William and Willie

C onstance met William Whitestead at Oxford University where they both worked on the student newspaper. They were immediately drawn to each other's small-town view of life.

William delighted Constance with stories of Stones End and Constance entertained him with life in The Cotswolds.

They marveled at small-town similarities no matter where they were in the world. The abundant supply of nosy neighbors. Obligatory fundraisers and bake sales. Community theater and annual flower shows all contributed to keeping the place they called home alive and thriving.

When they decided to marry, the decision about what continent to live on came easy for Constance.

William had no siblings and his parents died when he was young. So, the logical choice would have been to live in England where Constance would be surrounded by family and friends.

Constance had other ideas. She was excited at the prospect of living somewhere more progressive. And Stones End definitely kept up with the changing times more than the traditional Cotswolds. And it was a manageable distance from Manhattan!

They were married in the twelfth-century church of Saint Mary's in Swinbrook, Oxfordshire. William loved the ancient feel of the church. It brought to mind the Sword in the Stone, Knights of the Round Table and King Arthur. He thought it heightened the sense of romance for their wedding and adventure for their new life.

When William shared the images Saint Mary's conjured for him with Constance, she laughed. "Wrong century, my dear."

"Don't burst my bubble," was his playful reply.

They finished their studies at Oxford, headed for America and settled into Stones End. It was the same year Arthur arrived from Greece.

William joined a local investment firm and Constance opened the bookshop.

She was elated to find that the printshop in Stones End produced the local newspaper, *The Village Crier,* and made an immediate connection with Arthur and Uncle Charlie. They gladly accepted articles on her unique perspective of village life.

At first, villagers were skeptical of her outsider views but Constance's gentle humor won them over.

One year after they arrived, Constance gave birth to a son who was named after his father but everyone called Willie.

Constance and William were madly in love with each other, their new life and their first child.

One day, William found it hard to take a deep breath.

"You're too young to be out of breath," Constance joked. "My grandfather used to complain of that in his old age."

But when William felt like an anvil dropped on his chest, Constance called the doctor.

"My dear, I'll be fine. Just doing too much, I suspect. And I definitely don't need to see the doctor," his voice rising as Constance was already walking toward the phone.

The doctor scheduled a series of tests and when they were finished, Constance said, "And now the waiting game."

"I know, waiting is a misery. So how about this, we won't worry until we have something to worry about?"

"Deal," said Constance. But she did worry. William was wincing at times and having to sit down more frequently after small exertions.

The day of the results arrived.

"Big day. I hope they just give me a fistful of pills and I'll be right as rain."

"Don't worry, darling, we can handle whatever they throw at us."

When Dr. Watkins walked in, they knew instantly the news was not good.

"William, I'm afraid you have a serious condition that has caused significant deterioration to the walls of your heart."

William's face went ashen. "Are you saying I need heart surgery?" He whispered as though speaking louder would make the news worse.

"I'm sorrier than I can say but I'm afraid it's more critical than that. I've consulted with several of my colleagues and we all agree. The only course of action is a heart transplant."

They went numb. Never did they expect the news to be this bad.

"How can this be? I'm only 24." His voice sounded oddly strangled.

"You didn't do anything wrong, William. Most likely you were born with this condition."

His thoughts were crashing into one another. William was afraid Constance could read his mind. He walked to the window.

I won't die and leave Constance and Willie. I won't! A stranger's heart in my chest. How will it know how I feel about my family? God, how can you do this to me?

He heard an angry, violent scream. Was it in his mind or did it actually escape in his agony?

"A heart transplant," Constance said wringing her hands. "A fairly new procedure, isn't it? When was the first one performed?"

"1968."

"Only 11 years ago. Have they perfected the surgery?"

"I know what you're thinking, Constance. But the reality is it's William's only hope. The more important consideration is finding William a healthy heart. I have notified the medical community of our need but I'm afraid it's a waiting game."

"How long a wait can we expect?" asked William.

"No way to tell, I'm afraid."

"So, this could take months?" said Constance.

"Yes. But please, let's stay optimistic. It could also be as soon as tomorrow. In the meantime, we need to check William into the hospital where we can monitor his condition."

William asked Dr. Watkins if he and Constance could have a moment alone.

Before Constance could start, William said, "I'm going to say, no, before you ask, my dear. I know you will want to care for me at home but I simply cannot burden you like that. You have Willie to care for."

"William, you will not be a burden, not to me," she said, choking on her tears. "Can you imagine if this takes months? Or even a year? How could we bear to be apart that long?"

"This is a shock but let's not dwell on the worst case. Take it a day at a time. We can get through this."

Constance hated this plan. She couldn't bear the thought of their little family being separated. She knew William would worry if his care fell to her. So, in the end, Constance agreed and William was admitted into the hospital within a few hours.

Constance's time and energy were stretched to the max. She juggled working at the bookshop, taking care of Willie and spending every spare moment at the hospital with William. She was adamant that William not miss a day with their son, so Willie and his overstuffed diaper bag were always in tow.

Coffee and adrenaline were the only things keeping her upright and moving. Her nerves were shot as day by day she watched William grow weaker.

Her friends in the village were frantic with worry and constantly offering help. "How can the poor thing manage?" The question on everyone's lips.

Arthur visited the hospital every day on his way home from work offering what little support he could to William and hoping to give Constance a dinner break.

The tragic day came after just one month.

Arthur first saw Willie in his bassinet at the foot of the bed. Constance was squeezed in next to William. She was holding his hand and stroking his hair. It seemed such a tender scene Arthur almost turned to leave.

Then he noticed Constance crying softly and he knew. William was gone.

His instincts told him to get mother and child home but as Arthur watched the sorrowful scene, he felt his presence was intruding on this family's last moments. So, he stepped into the hall and waited.

In the blink of an eye, maybe two, the hospital staff came rushing down the hallway. They nodded toward Arthur.

He entered the room and took hold of Constance's hand. Her sorrow pierced his soul. Then he picked up Willie's bassinet and looking at this tiny child, Arthur thought, *poor little fellow. Facing life without Dad.*

Arthur gathered mother and son to him and led them from the beloved husband and father.

Once he got them home, it was obvious to Arthur that Constance was in no shape to care for Willie. He called the only person who popped into his head. He called Mrs. Kruchinski.

Mrs. Kruchinski came on the run and immediately took charge. She changed and fed Willie, made Constance a cup of tea and scurried back to the kitchen to prepare dinner.

She called Karl and told him to bring her night things. She was staying with Constance. Which is what she did for a solid week until Constance rallied.

The friendship between Arthur and Constance grew closer after William's death. He came by often to check on her and Willie. She would invite him to stay for dinner but he always declined. He didn't want tongues wagging in the village. The last thing Constance needed was to be the topic of gossip.

Constance was grateful for Arthur's visits. "If it wasn't for you, Arthur, I would surely have gone mad."

CHAPTER 26
Constance and Willie

Now we all know how life can bring us to our knees. As it turned out, Constance had one more cross to bear.

It was Christmas vacation. Willie was 12 years old and begging his mother to go ice skating on the pond with his friends.

"No, you don't, you crazy child. It's not nearly cold enough to be fully frozen. It's a good day to stay home and finish your report for school. It's due next week, you know."

While Constance was at the bookshop, Willie's friends came calling and his mother's warning went right out of his head. He grabbed his skates from the hall closet and took off for the pond.

They were enjoying a fine skate when the sun came out midafternoon and they heard the first crack.

"Get off the ice! She's cracking," yelled Sammy Collins. The boys skated hard and fast for the shore 30 yards away. Willie had 20 yards to go when he heard the second crack. It was a thunderous sound. In a split second, he disappeared through a large black hole.

The boys were shaken. Some fought back tears, others stood wet-faced. Poor Eddie Nunez bit his lip bloody. Someone kept screaming Willie's name. Billy Reynolds clamped his eyes shut and balled up his fists as though ready to fight whatever demon took their friend.

Sammy yelled again. "Everyone lay down. Make a human

chain."

The boys obeyed. Sammy took the lead. But when they reached the hole in the ice, Willie was nowhere to be seen.

Mr. Johnson, the vet, had been driving by and saw what happened. He was running down from the road yelling for the boys to get off the ice.

He tied a rope around his waist and told the boys to hold on tightly. "When you feel my tug, pull me out as fast as you can."

With that, Mr. Johnson ran onto the ice and jumped through the hole where Willie disappeared.

The boys waited for what seemed an eternity. Finally, they felt the tug and began running hard gripping the rope with all their strength.

Mr. Johnson came through the hole in the ice like a breached whale. To their horror, he was alone.

It was about 3 pm when Constance decided to check on how Willie's report was coming.

When she went to hang up her coat in the hall closet, she noticed Willie's jacket and skates were missing. An alarm sounded. She flew out the door. Constance prayed out loud the entire trip to the pond, "Oh please, God, let him be safe."

When she arrived, Mr. Johnson was walking back over the ice. He was drenched to his skin and ice was forming on his mustache.

She scanned the crowd of boys for Willie. She couldn't see him. Constance's heart was pounding. She called out, "Willie! Willie!"

Mr. Johnson and the boys jerked their heads around. When she saw the horrified look on Mr. Johnson's face, she shook her head violently. "No, no. Please God, not Willie."

She screamed Willie's name over and over as though willing him to appear before her.

And then Constance stopped. The unspeakable truth hit. Her beautiful Willie was gone. She fell to her knees and let out a bone-chilling scream that was heard all the way back in the village.

Everyone instinctively grabbed their coats and ran into the street.

Walter called out, "Where did it come from?"

Arthur yelled, "The pond!"

They ran hard toward the dreaded pond. No one was prepared for the unbearable sorrow they found.

Constance was crumpled on her knees. Her arms wrapped around her waist. She was rocking back and forth saying over and over, "Oh God, please help me. God, help me."

Willie's friends were in shock. Parents gathered them up and took them away from the tragedy. Arthur threw his coat around Doc Johnson and put him in his truck with the heater on full blast.

Mrs. Kruchinski wrapped herself around Constance in a bear hug. "You cry, Constance. Cry until you can't cry anymore. I've got you."

CHAPTER 27
Constance Moves Forward

Willie's death snuffed out a brilliant, vibrant light in the village. Poor Father Peter was asked again and again, why would God let such a terrible thing happen? The old priest would just shake his head. He had no words of comfort.

Life felt one-dimensional. It was as though the village ate, drank and slept the tragedy. Every conversation centered around worry for Constance. "How will she ever survive this? First her beloved William and now her baby. It's too much to bear."

Father Peter called an emergency parish meeting to discuss how they could guide Constance through this crisis.

"One of our own is in deep trouble, my friends, and we must rally around her. We must be her strength and her hope. We must find a way to keep a light shining before her, so she doesn't fall into darkness." The priest paced the room, looking for ideas and volunteers.

"Food," Oscar called out. "Madge and I will make sure Constance is well-fed. She'll need to keep her strength up."

"And I don't think she should be alone right now," said Mrs. Kruchinski, and immediately organized a group of women to stay with Constance.

"Excellent, both of you. That's the spirit," said Father Peter.

"We'll need volunteers keeping The Page Turner open," called out Walter. "I'm in for taking shifts at the bookshop and will organize the rest of us to do the same. We can't let bankruptcy add to Constance's worries."

And one by one, they called out ways to help Constance. It was as if the village had wrapped a giant swaddling blanket around her.

Arthur checked on Constance every day to see what she needed as did Birdie who hardly left her side.

Father Peter was a daily visitor as well. He brought her communion and would sit for hours telling stories and parables, asking questions and urging her not to lose faith.

"It's impossible to understand God's plan for us at times like this. Please know this, Constance. God still has a plan for you. I'm here to help you find it."

After one week, Constance began walking in the park. After two weeks, she wandered into the bookshop to check on things. And after one month, Constance asked the congregation after Mass if they wouldn't mind staying for a moment. She had something to say.

Constance stood in front of her friends and felt her eyes glossy with tears.

"You might think these are tears of sorrow. But I assure you they are tears of joy. You see, with the tender care of all you good people, I climbed my way out of a very dark hole. A place I pray you never have to visit."

"Each time I felt myself giving up and falling back down, another of your hands would reach out to me. I could almost hear you saying: *Grab my hand, Constance, and don't let go.*"

"Thank you for your love and incredible friendship. I owe a

115

great debt to you all. I would never have emerged from such tragedy without your care. Never."

"To your credit and God's credit, I am ready to go forward in
life with hope."

"You will forever be in my prayers."

Well, there wasn't a dry eye in the house. Everyone rushed
out of the pews to hug Constance.

Yes, I'm going to make it.

CHAPTER 28
A Village Friendship

Everyone went back to their normal routines, except Arthur. He continued to worry about Constance on her own and would still check on her. Not every day, but once or twice a week.

Constance still invited Arthur to stay for dinner. Arthur still declined not wanting to shine a speculative light.

But years later when Oscar and Madge started their Thursday night gourmet dinners, Arthur thought it would be fun eating together at The Café. He was hopeful that eating out in public and not Constance's home would not cause undue gossip.

Their dinner conversations were wide-ranged and they were especially delighted to learn they both loved movies and agreed the old black and white ones were the best.

Arthur had a large movie collection and invited Constance over.

"Arthur, this is impressive. Oh my gosh, you have 'The Uninvited' and 'The Ghost and Mrs. Muir.' I love those movies."

"You can borrow any movie you like."

"I'd borrow them all but I don't have a VCR."

"Look, you have the Alastair Sim version of 'A Christmas Carol.' That's my absolute favorite. What do you say, let's watch it?"

And that started movie night. Constance would go over to Arthur's every Friday. Arthur would always make sure popcorn was ready. And Constance never showed up without a plate of brownies.

One Thursday night, Constance was running late for dinner at The Café. Arthur, who was waiting in her parlor, noticed a game on her bookshelf.

"Constance, do you play Scrabble? I love the game but never found anyone here to play with."

"Are you kidding me, Arthur? I adore the game and would be thrilled to have a Scrabble partner."

So, they reserved Sunday afternoons for rousing Scrabble games. Arthur and Constance were fiercely competitive players yet gracious losers. They loved their weekly games and the comfort of their decades-old friendship.

The villagers seemed hopeful that they might get together as a couple. Arthur and Constance assured them they were just friends.

"That may be so for Arthur," said Mrs. Kruchinski to anyone who would listen. "But I see how Constance looks at him lately and I think she is falling in love."

When Karl heard the rumor his wife was spreading, he was furious. He told her to stop her gossip immediately and not to encourage any hope in this direction.

"It's just a harmless observation, Karl."

"Arthur is a confirmed bachelor, and you know this to be true, Olga. Your meddling will only hurt Constance in the end and that woman doesn't deserve any more grief in her life."

So, Mrs. Kruchinski never mentioned it again. But the damage was done. Everyone in the village knew of Constance's new-found love for Arthur. Everyone, that is, except Arthur.

CHAPTER 29
Opening Pandora's Box

Father Gregory watched Arthur as he hunched forward. His arms were leaning on his legs and his expression was blank. His eyes held a distant stare. Arthur was traveling back through years of pain and regret.

He's summoning the courage to do battle with his past, thought Father Gregory.

"Take your time, Arthur, there's no hurry."

"No, it's time, Gregory. It's time to share this burden." And he began....

Arthur just turned 22 years old. He was still in Greece working at the printshop for the past four years. Uncle Charlie was thrilled with his work. By the end of the first year, he considered Arthur an expert. He was eagle-eye accurate at typesetting, learned to tame the cantankerous press and was a natural at charming the customers. So, when Uncle Charlie met the love of his life and moved to America, he was confident in leaving the business to Arthur.

As the new owner, Arthur was excited one day to get a large order from a prominent family in the area. Hoping they would spread the word of his excellent printing, Arthur handled the job personally including the delivery. He left nothing to chance.

The programs he was delivering were for Ana Felicia's singing debut hosted by her parents in two weeks. It was an evening event in the grand ballroom of their sprawling mansion.

Ana Felicia spent the past eight years under the tutelage of vocal coaches. Now, at the age of 18, she was an aspiring opera singer. Her family's wealth and prominence assured her some part, if not the lead, in next season's production of "La Boehme" at the opera house in Madrid.

As Arthur went to knock at the mansion delivery entrance, the door flew open and Ana Felicia rushed out. She crashed into Arthur, sending the box of programs flying.

"Oh no," Arthur shouted. "They'll be ruined."

Ana Felicia helped him gather the scattered programs.

"It's my fault. I'm so terribly sorry. Please forgive me," she repeated. Arthur was so annoyed with this clumsy girl he couldn't bring himself to graciously accept her apology.

As Ana Felicia handed Arthur the last soiled copy, he looked at her for the first time. Her beauty was so luminous he was sure an angel stood before him.

Ana Felicia was so distraught that Arthur may lose his job, she choked on tears.

"Please don't worry. I'll tell everyone it was my fault," she said.

Arthur didn't know what to do. She looked miserable.

"Please forgive me. I'm making such a mess of everything," she said.

"It's alright. The programs look fine. No harm done and no need for tears," said Arthur gently offering his handkerchief.

"And I'm completely forgetting my manners," Ana Felicia said dabbing her eyes.

"I'm Ana Felicia and these programs are for my singing debut which, I'm afraid, has made me a bundle of nerves," she said with a nervous laugh.

Arthur was shocked that she was the reclusive Ana Felicia. He had heard of her all his life. She was known to be the most beautiful girl in the village yet few ever caught a glimpse of her.

She was the only child of wealthy parents. They traveled throughout Europe regularly and were rarely home. When they were, Ana Felicia was never allowed off the estate unchaperoned.

"It's understandable," said Arthur.

"You're very kind. May I ask your name?"

Feeling suddenly clumsy in the presence of such elegance, he blurted: "Arthur. My name is Arthur and I'm sure your concert will be a smashing success."

"That's kind of you to say, Arthur. Are you familiar with opera?"

"Not too much. My aunt loves opera, though. Whenever we visit her, she plays opera records. It's the most beautiful music I ever heard."

Hoping to sound sophisticated, he added, "I plan to attend the opera one day."

"How lovely. May I repay your kindness and invite you to the concert? I know it's not like being at the opera but I plan to sing some opera."

Arthur was amused. He desperately wanted to say yes but knew her parents would be horrified with a tradesman at the gala.

"I would love nothing else. But I'm afraid I'd be a fish out of water in such rich company."

Ana Felicia didn't want to be rude. She guessed Arthur was right. Her parents would throw a fit.

After a thoughtful pause, she offered a hopeful solution.

"If it would be alright with you, Arthur, there's a secret gate I could leave open. It's at the far end of the garden hidden under a weeping willow. There's a bench just inside where you can watch and listen to the concert."

Arthur was thrilled. He'd see Ana Felicia again and hear her sing. The thought made his own heart sing.

"I don't know how long it will take before I can slip away, but if you wouldn't mind waiting, I'll come out to see you as soon as I can."

Arthur couldn't remember the bike ride back to his shop. He had just met a divine being. At one point he put his hand to his chest to make sure his heart beat normally again. He was sure this was what heaven felt like.

The rest of the day was a blur as Arthur shuffled around in a lovestruck trance. Panic set in when he left work.

I'll need a haircut. Shine my shoes. Give my suit a good brushing. Should I buy a new shirt? A manicure. I'll need a manicure to get the ink off. No, not in the budget. I'll just keep my hands out of sight.

He finally stopped his frenetic thoughts and laughed. There was no hurry. It was two weeks before the concert.

The next day, Arthur's mind was wrapped in daydreams of Ana Felicia. When he stopped the presses, she was standing before him. The sight of her made heart-stopping breathlessness wash over him.

There was an aura shimmering around her as though sunlight was escaping from her very being. She stood with the quiet elegance of a woman yet her expression flashed girlish delight.

Her scent hinted of jasmine on a hot summer night, her movement of a leaf lightly floating on a soft breeze, her eyes sparkled with the wonderment of the universe. Who was this standing before him? Woman or child? Temptress or innocent?

He knew right then and there he could fall in love with her.

Be careful, he heard his father's voice, *the heart is fickle.*

Arthur asked if she wanted to take a stroll. To his delight, she said yes.

They talked about everything and nothing and she laughed at his very lame jokes. Arthur felt as close to ecstasy as he could imagine.

The Picnic

Arthur and Ana Felicia spent as much time together as they could possibly steal away in the two weeks before the concert.

He hoped their relationship was progressing and longed for a more private setting than the park bench.

He suggested a picnic by the sea two days before the concert. He held his breath waiting for her answer. Yes! His joyful heart raced.

He spent almost a week's wages for food, flowers, a picnic basket and even splurged on what he hoped was a passable bottle of wine.

The much-anticipated picnic day arrived. Arthur and Ana Felicia climbed to the top of a rock ledge perched high above the Mediterranean Sea. It was Arthur's favorite place and offered them privacy.

When Ana Felicia saw their picnic spot, she seemed wary of the seclusion and started to fidget.

Arthur berated himself. *You're such a fool. You pushed her too fast.*

He quickly asked if she would prefer to move closer to the water where he knew they would be in full view of everyone.

She hesitated then seemed to be struck by the thoughtfulness of his offer. "No, Arthur, this is wonderful."

Ana Felicia insisted on setting out their lunch.

"What is in that secret bag you brought?" Arthur asked.

"It's a surprise," she replied. "Now, just lay back and don't peek."

Arthur happily stretched out on the blanket next to her. He had the sense of being a child again when life was lived closer to the ground and you noticed more of the world around you.

He closed his eyes and listened to the screeching conversations of seagulls. Wild orchids on a far-off ridge graced the air with whiffs of delicate scent. The sun warmed. The sea breeze cooled. It was perfect.

In a Greek paradise stretching only to the perimeter of their blanket, a blinding moment of happiness. He never wanted to leave.

"Lunch is served," Ana Felicia announced.

Arthur marveled at their dining table. Glistening grapes promising juicy bites sat in a white bowl with blue hand-painted flowers. A wet sheen covered the soft salty cheese which was laid on a silver tray and the bread warmed by the sun was nestled in a wicker basket. Flower petals of pink, white and yellow were strewn around their feast.

"Oh, how wonderful," said Arthur touching Ana Felicia's hand. "Let's eat. I'm starving."

Ana Felicia laughed and threw a napkin at him.

They ate and talked and played and talked. She tossed a grape that he tried to catch in his mouth and missed. He flicked a stray bit of bread from her lip. She leaned over and brushed back the hair from his eyes. Their conversation held the excitement of newlyweds. Their endearing gestures the familiarity of an old married couple.

They told each other about their families, their childhood, their passions. Ana Felicia's passion was, of course, music.

"It moves me, Arthur, like nothing else. When I sing, I enter a world where only beautiful music exists and it creates the illusion that everyone on Earth is happy. Does that sound crazy?"

"No, I completely understand. I get the same feeling when

I work with wood. When I pick up a piece of teak or cedar, the world and all its problems fade behind me. The scent of wood stirs something deep within me."

"Yes. You do understand."

Having eaten their fill, Arthur and Ana Felicia stretched out on the blanket. Arthur couldn't remember when he ever felt so relaxed in the presence of a woman. It was the profound feeling of being comfortable in his own skin.

"By the way, I love your name...Ana Felicia. It has a Spanish or maybe Italian flair to it. Most of all it sounds musical to me. Which I guess, is fitting."

"I love hearing that, Arthur. Actually, you're not far off. I'm named after both my grandmothers. My mother's mother was born in Spain and her name was Ana. My father's mother was born in Italy and was named Felicia."

Ana Felicia shared with Arthur the loneliness as an only child and how she envied him with his siblings.

"You must have friends."

"No friends, unfortunately. My parents brought school to me by hiring tutors. I'm never allowed off the estate alone. It's a miracle that I've been able to slip away these two weeks."

"I've been meaning to ask how you managed it."

"At first, it was easy. The place is in turmoil preparing for the concert. No one noticed. But one day my mother caught me coming back from the village."

"What did she say?"

"She asked where I had been. I simply told her that I had things to tend to and was certainly old enough to take care of them myself. Then I just turned and nonchalantly walked away."

"I'm proud of you," Arthur said touching her shoulder. "I have a feeling it didn't end there, though?"

"Surprisingly, it did. I was prepared to do battle but none came."

"Maybe she realized that you were finally grown up."

"Possible but not probable. I think she was momentarily stunned by my response," she laughed falling into Arthur.

"I hate the thought of you not having friends, Ana Felicia."

"I do visit my cousins from time to time. We always have a wonderful time but then it's time to go home. None of them live in Greece."

Arthur shared how he and his father repaired the schooner. He told her of the maiden voyage. "It was the best day of my life," he said, "until now."

"How is it that you work at the printshop and not at your father's boatyard?"

"I did work every summer at the boatyard with my father when I was a boy. He was a master carpenter and taught me everything I know."

"So that's where you get your love of wood."

"But when I turned 18, he and my mother wanted me to learn the printing trade, thinking it would offer me a better future. So, I went to work with my Uncle Charlie."

"Did you like the change?"

"Not at first. But I learned to like it very much. Uncle Charlie is a wonderful man and is very much like my father. He and my father are brothers and grew up in England."

"How did they both end up in Greece, of all places?"

"Their Aunt Millicent married a man from Greece. His name was Nick. He owned the printshop and the boatyard here."

"My father knew your Uncle Nick. He spoke of him highly."

"My father came to visit him and Aunt Millicent one summer. It's when he met my mother and fell in love. After they married, my father stayed and worked for Uncle Nick in the yard."

"So, your father chose the boatyard over the printshop?"

"Yes. With his passion for wood, it was the only choice. He built fishing boats."

"And your Uncle Charlie chose printing. Interesting. Two brothers, two vastly different careers."

"Yes, and the choice suited both of them to a T."

"It sounds like you were close to your father."

"Very. He was my best friend." Arthur turned his head away trying not to let sad memories creep into their day.

"My father knew your father as well. He respected him."

"Thank you."

Arthur stared out beyond the sea. She continued slowly.

"We were all saddened by his death. So young. So tragic. How are you and your family coping?"

"We're all fine," Arthur blurted out. Hearing his curtness, he added, "Thank you for your concern and kind words."

Ana Felicia sensed that the memory was still too raw for him. She decided to change the subject.

"How did your Uncle Charlie end up in Greece?"

"When my grandparents died, he moved to Greece to be near my father. Nick and Millicent never had kids. Millicent died first. So, when Uncle Nick died, he left my father the boatyard and Uncle Charlie the printshop."

"So, you still work with your Uncle Charlie? I'd like to meet him someday."

"Well, you'd have to go to America to meet Uncle Charlie. He met a woman from a small village there. She was vacationing in Greece and it was love at first sight for both of them."

"How beautiful."

"They fell in love and married."

"They were that sure from the beginning?"

"Yes, they were. She couldn't bring herself to leave her family. So, Uncle Charlie, who loved the small-town sound of her village, left me the business. He moved to America where he opened another printshop."

"Do you keep in touch with your uncle?"

"Yes, we write and talk often. He's like a second father to me."

"Love at first sight. How bewitching."

Then she looked at Arthur and said with such quiet confidence, "I felt the same way, the first time I looked at you, Arthur. You're the only person who makes me feel safe...and loved."

Her words filled his heart with profound joy.

He turned and said, "It was the same for me, Ana Felicia. You made my heart stop the first time I looked at you. I will always keep you safe and you will always have my love."

And then he kissed her. It was a most tender kiss that spoke of all the joys their future held.

Doubts Creep In

Arthur's best friend Dean started teasing him.

"You're floating on air these past two weeks, Arthur. What's going on?"

Arthur never shared details of his private life. It was the British in him, he supposed.

But his excitement won out. He'd be attending Ana Felicia's singing debut.

Dean's reaction puzzled him.

"Arthur, these rich girls are out of our league. You're falling in love with her, aren't you?"

Arthur didn't reply.

"Trust me, my friend, this will end badly."

"I'm sure you're wrong, Dean," he said defensively.

Dean, always the realist, pressed him.

"Arthur, you're a tradesman. Ana Felicia is a filthy rich girl. Her parents would never allow you within a hundred feet of their only daughter."

"That is certainly a concern."

"I know you're a romantic kind of guy. But that stuff only happens in the movies. Just don't get your hopes up too high is all I'm saying."

Arthur didn't know if he was angry or confused. His heart was saying that Dean was dead wrong but his mind darkened with shadows of doubt.

The night before Ana Felicia's debut was a sleepless one for Arthur. He couldn't imagine how he was going to get through work the next day and still make it to the concert. But his great longing to see Ana Felicia carried him through the day and to the hidden garden gate.

Arthur arrived early. As he put his hand on the latch to the gate, Dean's warning haunted him.

He tried to shake it off but no such luck. *Maybe she forgot or changed her mind. Or maybe Dean is right and I'm just being a fool to think I would be allowed a glimpse into this lavish world of wealth and beauty.*

Then he imagined Ana Felicia's face in front of him. He could almost feel her lips on his. He turned the latch. It opened. *She remembered!*

Ana Felicia's Debut

He crept in and sat down on the bench against the far wall in the garden. He placed the flowers he brought carefully next to him.

As he sat quietly in the shadows of the garden, Arthur was struck with the grandeur of the estate. The front was shrouded in trees designed to offer privacy but the view from this vantage point was wide open. Rolling lawns, shrubs and bushes looking as though they stood for centuries. Fountains, stone patios and walkways leading to a hidden portico, a pergola, a dozen trellises. It was magnificent, manicured and exuded wealth and elegance.

The mansion was built of white stone and gleamed against the night sky. He looked up to the second floor. *Oh my God, there must be a dozen or so bedrooms in this place.*

Each bedroom had floor-to-ceiling French doors that led out to a balcony edged with wrought iron fencing. He marveled that every light in the house was on making windows appear warm and friendly. *Their electric bill must be astronomical. Mom would have had a fit seeing this.*

He wondered if Ana Felicia's father was a self-made man or if he inherited his fortune. He concluded the latter. Her father's arrogance was legendary. It spoke of entitlements that come only from old money.

Arthur knew he was early and decided to go snooping. Keeping to the shadows of the trees, he walked around. His jaw tightened when he reached the edge of the house. The sign on the side door read: Servants Entrance. He recognized it as the line between the two worlds. The rich and famous and the poor and unknown. He knew which side he lived on.

He curiosity was snuffed out. He shuffled back to the bench.

From his seat against the back wall, he could see the guests taking their seats in the lavishly decorated hall.

There must have been at least 100 people. Each man regal, proper and polite. Each woman of every age coiffed, cultured and accustomed to a life of luxury, charm and without much struggle to make a living.

Arthur was in awe of how exquisitely everyone was dressed. The women's gowns shimmered in the light from the grand chandeliers and the men all looked smart in their tuxedos.

The opulent room appeared as a verdant indoor garden. Potted palms and rose bushes lined the walls. Low planters bursting with daffodils, petunias and orchids outlined the marble floor. And he could smell the ambrosial scent from the lilac bushes forming an archway into the great hall.

Just then, he looked at his worn suit and wished he had, at least, bought a flower for his lapel.

Suddenly, Arthur had the sense of washing up on an unfamiliar shore. He felt shabby and out-of-place. Dean's advice to stay realistic and remember his station in life pushed into his thoughts.

This world is beyond my reach. I should go home before I make a fool of myself.

Arthur stood to leave. But as he put his hand on the garden gate, the music in the great hall unfolded on the sea breeze. The sheer power of it pulled him back to the bench.

Ana Felicia made her grand entrance. Arthur focused as her presence filled the room.

The orchestra came to attention waiting for the applause to end. Violin and cello bows poised in mid-air, lips almost touching the mouthpieces of the horns, cymbals held wide.

Arthur could feel the tension and worried if it affected Ana Felicia. But she stood erect with calm elegance. She was positively radiant.

She was enveloped in a silver gown that created the illusion of moving water when she walked. Her hair was pinned up in a sophisticated French twist and strands of tiny white pearls hung down to her lily-white shoulders.

The music began and filled the very air he breathed. It started slow. Violin bows touching lightly to string. Flutes in long drawn out notes. Cellos dropped in. French horns and trumpets cut the air. Cymbals crashed. It was haunting, aching. Reverberating in Arthur's chest and head, touching his soul.

Ana Felicia stepped forward and began to sing.

Arthur put his hand to his chest barely able to breathe. Her voice was extraordinary. Pure and piercing. One moment light as a snowflake's descent then soaring to the heavens with exhilarating power. It felt as though time stopped as the universe listened to her rapturous voice.

The audience was mesmerized. Held by her spell, they witnessed the birth of a new opera star. One who would be immortalized by the world.

Arthur sat for the entire hour of the concert without moving. He was sure his heart had stopped beating.

The concert ended. Guests burst from their seats. The standing ovation wouldn't stop.

Ana Felicia graciously gave a deep elegant bow and stood quietly thanking guests.

She did it, he thought. *She was magnificent. They all love her.*

Old family friends, all of them new fans, enveloped Ana Felicia each vying for her attention.

They are all so beautiful. It was like a fairy tale. He never wanted this moment to end.

Just then, Ana Felicia looked over her shoulder into the garden to the exact spot he was standing. Arthur knew she couldn't see him from where he stood in the shadows. But it felt as though their eyes locked.

It was that exact moment when the contrast of where she was standing and where he was standing struck him. He knew Dean was right.

She stood in a luxurious world filled with beautiful people and elegant music. Loved by all. He stood in the shadows of a wet garden. A complete nobody.

He looked down at the suit he spent an hour pressing and brushing. To his horror, it was completely wrinkled from sitting in the damp night air. The shoes he polished were now caked with mud. And despite scrubbing his hands till they bled, there were still traces of black ink from the presses.

Arthur looked one last time into the extravagant room that was Ana Felicia's world. Ana Felicia had turned back to her guests. Then he, too, turned and walked into the shadows of the night.

As he closed the gate to Ana Felicia's world, he heard his father's voice. "Never trust your heart, Arthur, always go with your gut...." And his gut was telling him to run as fast as he could.

A Night of Anguish

Arthur did not go home after the concert. He walked all night in the shadows. They offered him little comfort in hiding his heartbreak, his humiliation.

He reasoned she belonged in that world, deserved the beauty and attention it lavished upon her. He simply would never fit in. He would be destined for a life as an afterthought by her family, friends and eventually Ana Felicia herself.

His real fear was that Ana Felicia would grow tired of him. Or worse, embarrassed of her lowly husband whose world was a shabby boatyard and struggling printshop. That, he knew, was something he couldn't bear.

Nor could he bear to imagine Ana Felicia in his world. Living in his one-room apartment scraping together money at the end of each week made him cringe.

His romantic thoughts of yesterday were transformed into fear today. They were no longer thoughts of love but of protecting Ana Felicia from a life of drudgery.

Best to make a clean break of it. He could think of no other way. He felt his heart would never beat again.

It was nearly dawn. Arthur headed home. He spent the entire night vacillating back and forth between running back to Ana Felicia and standing firm to his decision. The raw emotion drained him.

He put his head on his pillow with only one thought, *I can't stay in this village a day longer.*

When he got up, he would call the editor of the newspaper who was always offering to buy him out. He'd sell the business.

He would explain to his siblings that he decided to move to America to live with Uncle Charlie. They could send him his share of the boatyard if they ever saw a decent profit.

Arthur had enough money for passage to America. And the final task was to write Ana Felicia a letter. With a plan in place, Arthur finally allowed himself to sleep.

CHAPTER 30
The Burning Question

Arthur stopped, too tired to go on. Clearly, opening old wounds was exhausting.

"How awful for you, my friend. How awful for Ana Felicia," said Father Gregory.

"How could I have left her, Gregory? She's the only woman I ever loved and I just left her. Why didn't I fight for her?"

"That's a complicated question, Arthur. There are so many things to consider. Your youth, for one. We tend to make decisions for the wrong reasons when we're young."

"Are you saying I made the wrong decision?"

"Not at all. A lot was going against you two. Vastly different backgrounds and lifestyles. That would seriously handicap your future. Not to mention, careers at the opposite ends of the spectrum."

"Very true."

"Then there was the matter of her parents' reaction. If they disapproved, there would be a lifelong battle. One, I'm afraid, would eventually declare a winner and loser."

"It sounds like you're saying my decision to leave was right."

"I'm afraid the right or wrong of it, Arthur, is for you to figure out. But I can tell you this, I know you to be a good man. And I believe that somewhere deep inside, you know the answer to your burning question."

CEIL WARREN

"Well, I'm at a loss."

"I suspect the answer is right under your nose. It may be time to open the letter, my friend."

After arguing with George all morning, Arthur was not up for another debate. So, he said, with as much conviction as he could muster, "I've decided not to open the letter, Gregory. And before you jump all over me, hear me out, please."

Father Gregory opened his mouth ready to express his concern but nodded instead.

"I've had a truly blessed life, filled with the love of good friends and an occupation I still find fascinating after all these years."

"You are blessed, Arthur."

"And as though all of that wasn't enough, I also possess a tender memory which has sustained me my whole life. And for me, it's enough. It's all I need."

"Are you sure?"

"Yes. I've decided not to be greedy and tempt fate. A fate that may cause me to lose my memories. I'm not opening the letter and that's my final decision. Best to let things be."

Father Gregory knew with a certainty he rarely felt that Arthur was making the wrong decision. But how to change his mind?

"Arthur, you have been living in the shadows long enough. You stood in the shadows at Ana Felicia's concert. Your reason for leaving her and your homeland, more shadows. Even your

140

memories have been shrouded."

"I've heard all this from George."

"Arthur, listen to me. The trick to life is to keep the sun on your face and the shadows behind you. It's time to come out of the shadows. Open the letter, Arthur. Turn toward the sun."

"George has been hounding me all morning to do just that," said Arthur in a defeated voice.

"Well, considering we both know George is your conscience, I say listen to him. Open the letter."

Mounting a final resistance, Arthur said, "Suppose the letter says she hates me, or worse, she never loved me? I'll lose my memories, Gregory."

"Trust me, Arthur, you can handle whatever is in that letter. The real issue here is that you simply cannot go on in the state you're in. You know it and I know it. And even George knows it."

That's it, Arthur thought. *I'm out of arguments.*

CHAPTER 31
An Unexpected Visitor

As Arthur went to get the letter, his head jerked in the direction of the path.

"Oh, who's this now?"

"Someone with very bad timing," Father Gregory muttered.

Only this time, the visitor was not only a surprise but a total shock.

Slapping his hand to his chest, Arthur called out, "Aristotle, is that you?"

As his brother came closer, Arthur spread his arms wide. "It is you! What on God's good Earth brings you to America?"

"Can't a man visit his kid brother?"

"You have a brother?" said a bug-eyed Father Gregory.

"Yes, yes, he's standing right in front of you."

"Aristotle, you're not bringing bad news about Zoe or Emily, are you?"

"Who are Zoe and Emily?" asked Father Gregory.

"Our sisters," answered Aristotle.

"You have a sister?" blurted Father Gregory, eyes still bugged.

"Two," said Arthur.

"You're a dark horse, Arthur Covington, a dark horse, indeed," Father Gregory said scratching his head.

"What's to eat, brother of mine? I'm starving." Aristotle rubbed his grumbling stomach.

"I'll cook us a Greek feast!" announced Arthur. "Let's talk in the kitchen."

Father Gregory moved toward the front door. Aristotle grabbed his sleeve holding him in place.

"We'll wait out here for you, Arthur, where we can enjoy your beautiful river. Just call us when the food is ready."

"That's fine, Aristotle. Give you a chance to get to know my very dear friend, Father Gregory. But no telling tales out of school, you two."

"Your secrets are safe with me, Arthur," Father Gregory said with a laugh.

"Not me, brother. I intend to spill my guts."

When Arthur was out of view, Aristotle abruptly turned to Father Gregory. "I desperately need to talk to you, Father."

"Yes, of course, Aristotle. By the way, do you go by Aristotle or Ari?"

"Everyone, except Arthur, calls me Ari."

"How is it that a British man ended up with such a wonderful Greek name, Ari?"

"We're not British, Father, we're Greek. Arthur never told you?"

"As a matter of fact, he's never spoken about his childhood."

Father Gregory sat scratching his head. Then, he got up, went to the front door and yelled to Arthur, "You're Greek!"

"Yes," Arthur yelled back.

"Not British?"

"No, whatever made you think I was British?"

"Mrs. Kruchinski has been telling everyone that you're a Brit. For years."

"Ah, yes, she does think that."

"And you never corrected her!"

"No, it's my little joke, knowing that she is wrong for once."

"Father!" Ari said urgently.

"Yes, yes, Ari. You'll have to forgive me but one of the foundations of my world has just been ripped out from under me. Arthur is Greek and has a brother and two sisters."

"Father!"

"Of course, Ari. What is it you need to discuss?"

"Did Arthur ever tell you about Ana Felicia?"

"Yes, as a matter of fact, just moments ago."

"And he didn't mention that their love affair took place

in Greece?"

"No, he didn't. I just assumed they were in England. How is it that you know about Ana Felicia, Ari? Arthur said he never told another living soul."

"Because I was there the night of her debut. I was hired as a waiter for the party. What did Arthur tell you about why he left the concert?"

Ari sensed that Father Gregory was reluctant to share what Arthur told him in confidence. So, he asked instead, "Did he tell you about his meeting in the garden that night with Ana Felicia's father?"

"My word. No. He didn't mention it."

"I'm not surprised he left that part out. It was terrible, Father, really terrible."

And Ari explained.

"After the concert, I went into the garden for a smoke. I stayed hidden because I saw Ana Felicia's father and another man walk toward the back of the garden."

"What did they want?"

"They started speaking to Arthur. Ana Felicia's father was informed just that day of their affair. And the guy there with her father revealed the secret."

Father Gregory held his hand to his mouth.

"Apparently, this guy wanted to marry Ana Felicia and was planning to approach her father for her hand. The arrangement was expected and so the man was shocked when one day he saw Ana Felicia out with Arthur."

"A prearranged marriage?"

"Sounds like it. He started to follow them every day and when he realized that something was developing, he brought the news to Ana Felicia's father."

"Her father knew?"

"Yep. And he was furious. He demanded that Arthur stop seeing his daughter. He said Ana Felicia's hand was already promised in marriage to someone of his choosing. And here, Father, he gave Arthur a murderous look."

"Poor Arthur."

"He told Arthur that Ana Felicia was going to be a famous opera star and simply would not have time for the likes of someone like Arthur."

"Oh, Ari."

"And then, Father, he threatened Arthur. I'll never forget what he said. 'If you ever see my daughter again, I will not only destroy your life but the lives of your brother and sisters.' His final words."

"So, he was a bully."

"Big time. Then the man promised Ana Felicia's hand chimed in. 'Look at you, in your wrinkled suit and dirty shoes and hands. Ana Felicia will marry me and I will give her the world. What could you ever offer her?'"

"And with that, they turned and went off laughing as if the thought of Arthur and Ana Felicia as a couple was the biggest joke in the world."

"They humiliated him, Ari."

"Yes. But Arthur rallied, Father, and he did something I'll remember to the day I die. He called out after them, 'My name is Arthur Covington,' he said in a loud voice."

"What did her father do?"

"He turned around looking ferocious like a lion ready to pounce. 'What did you say?' he spat out in a way that would have stopped any man in his tracks. But not Arthur, Father, not my brother."

"Good for Arthur." Father Gregory punched his fist in the air.

"Arthur stood his ground and repeated, 'My name is Arthur Covington, sir. I wanted you to know the name of the man who loves your daughter more than life itself.'"

"Wow. That took courage."

"It gets better. Arthur then turned to the man with Ana Felicia's father. 'And to answer your question of what I could possibly offer Ana Felicia. The answer is my love.'"

"Bravo, Arthur," Father Gregory said, slapping his hand to his knee so hard Ari was sure he caused a fracture.

"Unfortunately, Arthur's grand moment was short-lived. The man's reply was laughter. It had a cruel sound to it. 'Love,' he said as though it were a dirty word. 'As if that would ever be enough for someone as magnificent as Ana Felicia.' And with that, he turned abruptly and walked toward the mansion."

"What a wretched man."

"And then a curious thing happened. Ana Felicia's father didn't leave immediately. He stood staring at Arthur. Oh, it was just a moment or two but I could tell Arthur's words clearly shocked him. I was sure he was going to say something. But, no. In the end, he just turned and walked away."

"What happened next?"

"Arthur took a long look at Ana Felicia in the ballroom. Then he left."

"His heart must have been broken."

"No, Father, Arthur's heart wasn't broken. It was destroyed."

"Her father knew, Ari. In those few moments, he stood looking at Arthur. He knew he was robbing his daughter of a lifetime of love and happiness."

"Yeah, Father, I agree. But in spite of knowing, he still sold out her dream for his manipulation."

"What happened then?"

"The two men stopped to talk before they went into the house, so I couldn't go to Arthur right away. When they finally went in, I raced to the back of the garden. He was gone. I ran through the streets all night looking for him."

"You didn't find him?"

"No. I finally gave up about 4 am. As I walked by the printshop, I couldn't believe what I saw. Ana Felicia was slipping an envelope under the door."

"Did you speak to her?"

"No. But I was angry. *She should leave Arthur alone,* I thought. And then I did a terrible thing, Father. I had Arthur's spare key to the shop. After she left, I opened the door and took the letter."

Father Gregory grabbed Ari's arm. "You did what?"

"I know, I know. But I thought at the time it was for the best. Her father was a ruthless, cruel man and no doubt powerful enough to make good on his threat."

"Ari, are you telling me you never gave your brother Ana Felicia's letter?" Father Gregory sat in jaw-hanging shock.

"It gets worse, Father."

Father Gregory held his hand tight against his forehead. "I don't know about that, Ari, this is pretty bad."

"After all these years, Ana Felicia got in touch about a month ago. It was easy enough for her to find me since I've been in the same place my whole life."

"What did she want?"

"Arthur's address. As we got talking, she said that there was something she needed to ask Arthur. She planned to visit him but didn't want to be rude and just show up."

"Obviously, you gave her the address."

"Yes. But once I heard she was coming, I knew I had to get

here first and give Arthur the letter."

"Oh my gosh. Ana Felicia is coming to Stones End!"

"Shhhh, Father, Arthur will hear you."

"When is she coming?"

"Don't worry, Father. Arthur knows about this. Ana Felicia sent him a letter about getting together...."

And before he could finish, Father Gregory blurted out in a high-pitched voice, "He's never opened the letter, Ari. It's still on his kitchen table. He doesn't know she's coming!"

Ari jumped up and screamed, "Sitting on his table...Ana Felicia is coming today!"

Arthur came running out of the house to see what all the yelling was about. Father Gregory held his hands to his head. "My goodness. We're in trouble, Arthur. We are in big trouble."

Arthur's eyebrows shot straight up. "Gregory, what on Earth are you talking about?"

"It's my fault, Arthur. It's all my fault," said Ari, holding both hands over his heart.

Arthur's eyes narrowed. "What the dickens are you two talking about?"

And Ari and Father Gregory yelled in unison. "Ana Felicia is coming. Here. Today!"

Arthur grabbed his chest, fell backward and landed right smack on George.

"Oh God, we broke him. We broke Arthur."

"He's not broken. Arthur, Arthur, are you alright?"

"It's no use, Father. We broke him."

"Stop saying that and help me get him up."

"Arthur. Snap out of it!"

Arthur raked his hands through his hair. "I desperately need a haircut. Aristotle, go in my closet and get my blue suit."

"Arthur, stop," said Father Gregory. "There's something more you need to know."

"I couldn't take any more surprises today, Gregory," Arthur said with a nervous laugh. "Whatever it is will have to wait."

"No, this can't wait."

Ari came flying out of the house with Arthur's suit in hand. "Arthur, this suit won't do. It won't do at all."

"What's wrong with my suit?"

"Stop right now, the both of you!"

Father Gregory stood deadly still. Then he turned to Ari and said, "Tell him."

"Tell me, tell me what?"

"There's a letter, Arthur...."

"Oh my gosh, I completely forgot about the letter on the kitchen table."

"No, not that letter," Father Gregory cried out.

"There's another letter?"

Father Gregory looked at Ari and repeated. "Tell him."

Ari dragged Arthur into the parlor and began relating what he had done.

He told him how he was in the garden that night and overheard what Ana Felicia's father had said to him. What her future husband said as well.

Arthur flinched at the thought of someone witnessing his humiliation, his shame. "That's enough, Ari. I can't bear anymore."

"Please, Arthur," said Father Gregory urgently. "There's something you need to know."

Arthur slumped into the couch completely overwhelmed.

"Go on, Ari," said Father Gregory. "Tell him about the letter."

When Ari finished relating what he had done, Arthur sat in disbelief. He handed Arthur the letter Ana Felicia had written 40 years ago. And without uttering a word, Arthur rose, went upstairs to his bedroom and closed the door.

"Oh God, what do we do now?"

"I suggest we eat the wonderful lunch Arthur made for us," Father Gregory said through clenched teeth.

"You can eat at a time like this?"

"It's called stress eating, Ari, and right now, I'm about as stressed as a person could be. So, come, sit down and eat your bloody lunch!"

CHAPTER 32
Opening the Letters

Arthur sat on the side of his bed. *Letters. Always getting letters. First my mother's letter, then the letter on the kitchen table, which I still must read, and now this one, 40 years late.*

He wondered. Was it a Dear John letter? Was she angry because he left her? Or was it a love letter that would have sent Arthur running back to her?

He couldn't help but think: *Did Aristotle rob me of my chance at happiness?*

Taking a deep breath, he opened the letter.

My darling Arthur,

I love you, my dearest.

I was heartbroken to find you had gone. I found your beautiful flowers, so I knew you were there.

At first, I couldn't bear to think of why you had left but I believe I now know. You simply did not see yourself in my world.

Arthur, all this wealth and luxury isn't real. The only thing that is real and matters in this world is love, our love. We can find a way to fit into each other's worlds. I'm certain of it.

Please don't give up on us. I don't want to imagine

a life without you, my love.

I'm so frightened with all that is in my future and I need you to guide me through it, Arthur. I need to feel your arms around me telling me everything will be alright.

I'm leaving for Madrid early Sunday morning. Please, can you meet me where we picnicked at 4 today?

All my love,

Ana Felicia

❦ ❦

Oh my God, she was waiting for me and I never showed up. I'm sorry, Ana Felicia, I'm so very sorry, my darling, for abandoning you.

Arthur's head dropped into his hands. *Is it possible I was wrong to leave?*

❦ ❦

Arthur came into the kitchen and without saying a word, snatched the letter from the table and went back to his room and closed the door for a second time.

"This is hopeful," said Father Gregory.

"How do you mean?"

"He's reading the second letter. Before he was dreading what was in it."

"Sorry, Father, I'm not following you."

"Don't you see, Ari? Arthur has finally made up his mind. He wants to see what the future holds."

"I always regretted taking that letter. I wondered my whole life if I robbed Arthur and Ana Felicia of married life together. So, if these two crazy kids get a second chance, I will be the happiest man in the world."

"Will Arthur tell us what is in the two letters, do you think?" asked Ari.

"Not a snowball's chance in hell."

My dearest Arthur,

So many years have passed since our parting...a whole lifetime of them. I have thought of you often through the years, more often than I probably should admit.

Please know, Arthur, that I never blamed you for leaving me that night. If I knew what life held for me, I would have run too. Not that my life has been terrible. I raised two beautiful children whom I adore.

I don't know if you heard, but my husband died last year. I am also retiring. My final performance will be in two months at The Met in New York.

So, as I find myself once again facing a strange new chapter in life, I naturally thought of you because you were there at the start.

Arthur, may I beg you to indulge an old lady and grant me a visit? There is something I would like to ask you. Only this time, I will come to you.

I arrive in New York early August. Once I tend to the preparations for my finale, I can come visit with you. Shall we say September 1 at 7 pm?

I am looking forward with the greatest anticipation to our reunion.

Yours,

Ana Felicia

Arthur came into the kitchen and sat down at the table.

"So?" said Ari.

"She wants to ask me a question."

"This is it, my brother. She's going to ask you to marry her. You two star-crossed lovers are finally going to get your happy ending."

A grinning Father Gregory gave Arthur a congratulatory slap on the back. Ari grabbed his brother in a bear hug that lifted him clear off the floor.

CHAPTER 33
Preparing for Ana Felicia's Visit

"Well, what are we waiting for?" asked Father Gregory. "We've got a million things to do before she gets here. How much time do we have?"

"What?" Arthur was holding his folded hands on the top of his head staring out at nothing.

"Time, time. What time is she coming?"

"7 pm."

"What time is it now?" asked Ari.

"It's 1!" yelled Father Gregory.

"Gregory, calm down. Six hours is plenty of time," said Arthur.

"Really, Arthur. You have to get a haircut," said Father Gregory.

"And buy a new suit, shirt, tie and shoes," added Ari.

"Flowers. You'll need to present Ana Felicia with flowers when she arrives," said Father Gregory.

"And dinner. What are you going to do about dinner? I suggest you eat here. So you have privacy," said Ari.

"Good idea," said Father Gregory. "We'll order dinner from The Café and have Oscar deliver it right before 7."

"Do you have any wine in the house, or better yet, champagne to celebrate?" asked Ari.

Arthur clasped his hands to stop the trembling.

"We're in trouble here, boys. We need reinforcements."

"You're right, Arthur. You're absolutely right. We need Mrs. Kruchinski."

"Sound the alarm, sound the alarm," Arthur yelled. The three men ran toward the village with Ari shouting over his shoulder, "Hold the fort down, George!"

When they told Mrs. Kruchinski what was going on, she stood looking blank for a full 10 seconds before shifting to full throttle.

"Leave everything to me," she said. "I will arrange for dinner, candlelight, linens, silverware and flowers for the table, and crystal glasses for the champagne."

"We need an emergency council meeting!" she yelled and ran out of the bakery without even locking up or putting up the Closed sign. Her parting words were, "You, go get a haircut. Now!"

CHAPTER 34
Ana Felicia Remembers

Packed and ready to leave for New York, Ana Felicia checked her purse one last time. *Plane ticket...check. Passport...check.* She paused. Glaring up at her was the letter to Arthur.

How do you approach someone after 40 years? Mindful doubts were waging war with heartfelt emotions.

She snapped her purse shut and headed for the Athens airport.

Ana Felicia arrived at The Met ready to prepare for her final concert. Costume fittings, endless meetings and brutally long rehearsals devoured every minute, giving her license to put off her decision about Arthur.

The last rehearsal of the day was finished. Ana Felicia walked off the stage and sat in the front row. Drained.

Everyone left for their evening break. She closed her eyes in the quiet of the opera house. Finally, a calm moment.

The history of the grand hall visited her. Pavarotti, Callas, Caruso, Fleming mesmerizing audiences, holding them captive. It felt like the center of the universe.

She still lived in awe of her part in that history. *Was I ever as great as the masters?* she wondered.

Her eyes opened wide as her reminiscing took a sudden turn. The future barged in like an uninvited guest. *What happens when it's over and I don't need to get out of bed? When I'm referred to as that old opera singer, what's her name? How will I fill my days for the next 30 or 40 years? What will become of me?*

The menacing guest answered: *You'll fade away.*

I need Arthur!

She jumped up and headed off with a single purpose. It was time to mail the letter.

The Manhattan crowds felt like an impenetrable jungle with no clear path. Hordes of suited workers snaked aggressively past thick flocks of tourists. Taxis menaced pedestrians and delivery bicycles threatened to knock over anything in their path.

Ana Felicia finally reached the mailbox...but stood frozen. Suddenly, mailing the letter proved harder than the thought of it.

Is this a good idea? I may be the last person on Earth Arthur wants to hear from. This crazy idea of mine! Can I trust my instincts? Will he welcome me in his life again? Lord, give me a sign.

Suddenly, a long screech of rubber, then the metal-grinding impact. Ten feet from Ana Felicia, a cab rear-ended a stretch limo. She jumped back and lost her footing. Unknown faces caught her before she hit the ground.

Making the sign of the cross, she looked upward acknowledging the heaven-sent sign. She tossed the letter into the box and headed for her hotel. *I definitely need a drink.*

Back in her suite at the Waldorf Astoria, she poured a glass of wine and put on music. The sun was low in the sky casting shards of light against the buildings, making them shimmer gold.

Sitting in a winged chair, Ana Felicia observed the perpetual movement of Park Avenue.

Elegantly dressed theatergoers shoulder-to-shoulder with the funkily clad nightclub crowd. Pretzel vendors pushing their carts. Professional dog walkers holding onto 10 leashes. Swarms of yellow taxis looking like angry bees.

Ana Felicia imagined living in the city. Rubbing elbows with artists, actors, captains of industry. Museums and Broadway in her own backyard. Manhattan fed off its own energy. Alive, vibrant, pulsating.

Vivaldi was trying his best to drown out the din of the city that never sleeps. She took a sip of wine and got lost in the memory of the young and dashing Arthur.

She remembered him as tall, broad-shouldered with a body toned from physical labor. His hair was dark, as thick as a carpet and had the endearing tendency to flop into his eyes.

Recalling Arthur's eyes, Ana Felicia felt the rise of goosebumps on her arm. His eyes could hold her in a trance with their smoldering intensity. Melt her heart with their kindness. And captivate her with their inquisitiveness.

From the moment they first met in Corso as kids, conversation came easy with Arthur. Ana Felicia had no experience in casual conversation. The only people she ever spoke with were her parents, tutors and servants. No casual talk with that lot.

Speaking with Arthur opened a whole new world for her. It was intimate, personal, almost raw. She told him things she had never entrusted to another person.

It felt as though she was not just sharing, but giving him her hopes, dreams, fears and passions. They spoke about their families, friends, island life, Arthur's existing career, her upcoming career.

She cherished the journey they traveled each day and hoped it would never end.

He was older than she, just by four years. She thought it gave him an air of worldliness. And it didn't hurt that she loved his smile.

Sometimes he gave an unsure lopsided grin, sometimes a full-toothed belly-laugh smile and when he was teasing, just the corners of his mouth would lift slightly.

The ringing phone interrupted Ana Felicia's memories.

"Hello, Monica, my darling. How are you?"

"I'm fine, Mother. More importantly, how are you? You must be going crazy with rehearsals. Your final performance. Are you nervous? I still can't believe you're retiring."

"It's unbelievable to me, too. But it's time."

"Any hint of your plans? I don't know why you are keeping such secrets."

"I'm not keeping secrets, my dear. I simply don't have them finalized yet."

"Really? You knew exactly what you wanted to do. Last time we talked."

"Yes, I do know but I have something to look into in New York. It may put my plans in motion. Why bother telling everyone now? If they don't come to pass, it will just cause disappointment."

"What are you looking into? New York of all places."

"Actually, I'm meeting an old friend to discuss an idea I have."

"Do I know her?"

"No, darling, you never met him. Hopefully, you will."

"Him? You said him! Oh my gosh, who is this mystery man?"

"Monica, please don't let your imagination run wild. He's just a childhood friend. From the island."

"I know you, Mother. When you don't speak of something, it's on purpose. And it always means you don't want anyone to know."

"Monica, please don't do this to me."

"Never mind, Mother. You're the one who brought it up."

"I know but I'm taking it back," she laughed.

"Not fair!"

"Please, darling, I have too much going on to contend with your snooping. You'll know all in due time. I promise."

"Alright, Mother. But the suspense is killing me."

"Talk soon, Luv."

Ana Felicia felt the need for a stronger libation. She poured herself a brandy. *The suspense is killing me, too.*

The amber glow of the brandy swirling into the glass brought her back to Greece, the secluded cliff above the Mediterranean and Arthur.

She relived the memory of their picnic many times over the decades. It was the day she and Arthur professed their love. The day when she knew she'd never be lonely again. She had someone to share life with.

Ana Felicia imagined the cliff as their own private dining room. The tall cypress stood as their walls, the picnic blanket their table and the gulls, sand crabs and sea turtles were their guests.

The sun hitting the sea mist from the crashing waves cast a gauzy haze over their picnic and a parade of rainbows for their entertainment.

Finally, a small slice of life that was her own. Deeply intimate and somehow forbidden but all hers.

Before meeting Arthur, Ana Felicia was sure she couldn't go through with her concert on their estate. Terror tightened her vocal cords, made her hands tremble and gave her sleepless nights.

But Arthur talked her off the ledge and onto the stage. His love and calm presence gave her confidence. The hall would be packed, but she was performing for an audience of one.

By the day of the concert, she was in control. One pressing challenge was finding a moment to unlock the garden gate for Arthur.

Her debut was triumphant. The audience burst from their seats yelling *Bravo* as the last note was sung. Ana Felicia was dazed by their responses.

The after-concert formalities dragged on at an agonizing pace. Long-winded congratulations, photoshoots, a steady stream of bouquets. Hugs, kisses, handshakes. It was hard appearing gracious. It was all too much.

Finally, the last guest departed. She raced to the back garden.

"Arthur, where are you?" Every fiber of her being was charged with excitement.

The surrounding garden emptiness confused her. He'd be there. He had to be. She looked wildly in every direction. Ran through the gate and searched the street beyond.

Back in the garden, the only sign of Arthur was the loose flowers he left on the bench. She held them tightly against her crushing disappointment.

He had left.

Suddenly, she panicked. She signed a contract just moments ago. She was leaving the day after tomorrow for Madrid. *Arthur, why didn't you wait?*

Her mind raced. *Did he hate the concert and didn't know how to tell me? Maybe he was tired, it was a long day for him too. One of the servants saw him and chased him away. Yes, that must be it.*

She had to see him. She didn't know how. With only one day left, she would find a way.

Ana Felicia held her hand to her forehead trying to calm the pounding in her head. She felt disoriented, stunned as she walked toward the house. *How could he leave?* She stopped. Her body tensed as she looked into the great hall.

Oh my God. Standing as still as the trees around her, a startling realization hit. *This was Arthur's view.* Her hand went to her heart. *He stood as an outsider looking in.*

And there in the shadows of the garden she knew. *He left because my world overwhelmed him. He left because he didn't know where he would fit in.*

His world was a simpler one driven only by work and family. Hers was a complicated web of social pressure, artistic excellence, stifling wealth and unreasonable expectations.

She covered her face with her hands. *I've lost him.*

Fighting off fears of never seeing Arthur again, Ana Felicia wrote a letter asking him to meet her the following day where they had picnicked. She knew if she saw him, they could work things out.

In the middle of the night, she tiptoed past the guardhouse careful not to wake the sleeping night watchman. Running the mile into the village, she reached the printshop tired and winded.

She looked around to make sure no one was watching, then slipped the letter to Arthur under the door.

As she turned for home, Mrs. Pappas' nasty black mutt appeared from around the side of the building. He was barking and snarling. She ran hard for the safety of the church. The dog was on her heels.

Her heart was pounding as she slammed the door of St. Gregory's, almost catching the dog's nose.

The church was dimly lit by the rows of prayer candles in their racks. She knelt down before the statue of the Blessed Mother and prayed aloud, "Please bring him back to me, Mary."

Returning home exhausted, Ana Felicia curled up on her bed. Sleep eluded her as her heart pined for Arthur. At breakfast, she absentmindedly moved food around her plate without ever taking a bite. She spent the day watching the clock, pacing, wringing her hands.

Finally, it was time to head to the cliff. She headed out ready to do battle with anyone who tried to stop her...even her parents, if necessary.

Her quick pace was driven by her emotions that were brutally bouncing between hope and heartbreak.

She reached the cliff sweaty and out of breath. It was deserted. She felt her confidence weaken but yelled defiantly into the wind, "He'll come."

Sitting on the sandy grass, Ana Felicia desperately hung onto thoughts of Arthur, the safety of his love and the promise of a life with the man she loved.

The moments stretched to an hour. Her confidence ebbed with the tide. *Please don't give up on us, Arthur.* She hugged her knees to her chest, wiping tears and midday sweat from her eyes.

After an hour, the small slice of life she called her own was like an apparition that had faded into nothingness.

Ana Felicia stood, futilely looked around one last time and

turned for home. *He's gone. Forever.*

The wind scattered the pieces of her heart over the crashing waves.

From the comfort of her winged chair overlooking Park Avenue, Ana Felicia sipped brandy and thought, *hopefully, not forever, Arthur.*

CHAPTER 35
The Second Emergency Council Meeting

Mrs. Kruchinski ran next door and yelled into the beauty parlor, "Emergency council meeting, now!"

Berris jumped right out of her sandals but came on the run leaving Mrs. Merriman with a wet head.

Then she ran all around town yelling, "Emergency council meeting, now!"

Father Gregory and Ari were sticking to her like flypaper.

"Father, go find Caroline and Birdie. They must be at the meeting. And Martin, too."

"We're on it," said Father Gregory and he and Ari took off like they were shot out of a cannon.

Mrs. Kruchinski erupted through the door of The Café cherry-cheeked and puffing like a locomotive. She plopped down on the first seat she could find.

Madge ran to her. "Olga, whatever is the matter? You look like you just ran an uphill marathon."

"Ana Felicia is coming to ask Arthur to marry her! Here! Tonight! That's what was in the letter!"

"Olga, Arthur is finally getting his happy ending!" She burst into a tearful fit.

"Madge, are you crying?" asked Oscar, coming out of the storage room balancing a stack of take-out boxes.

Madge told Oscar the news. The boxes went into the air. He shouted, "Good for Arthur. Can't wait to congratulate him."

Just then, the door to The Café crashed open and the backup troops charged in.

Mrs. Kruchinski took command. "Good, we're all here except Walter who is giving Arthur a haircut and Karl who is in the middle of a landscape job."

She told them about the letter and that Ana Felicia was coming to ask Arthur to marry her.

"Wait a minute," said Father Gregory. "To be precise, Ana Felicia said she wanted to ask Arthur a question. The letter did not mention marriage."

"What other question could she possibly want to ask?" said Caroline.

"I agree that's what Ana Felicia is going to ask," said Father Gregory. "Just saying, that's all."

"To continue," Mrs. Kruchinski said, giving Father Gregory a squinty-eyed look. "We need to prepare for Ana Felicia's visit. Here's the list."

"First, dinner," and she was interrupted by Oscar.

"I'm already on it. Roast rack of lamb with mint jelly, rosemary potatoes and asparagus." And then he added, "Madge, my partner in crime, I need your help to pull this off."

"I've got your back, my dear."

"Excellent," said Mrs. Kruchinski.

"Next, flowers."

Another interruption, this time by Constance. "A corsage for Ana Felicia, a bouquet for the table and a flower for Arthur's lapel."

"Perfect," said Mrs. Kruchinski.

Berris jumped in next. "When Arthur is finished getting his haircut, have him come over to the beauty parlor. I'll get that ink off his hands."

"And I'll take the table setting," said Mrs. Kruchinski.

"Now who will be in charge of the wine?" she asked.

"I'll take that one," said Birdie. Nervous sideways glances shot around the table.

"You can wipe the worried looks off your faces. I know my wine."

Deputy Caroline chimed in. "And I'll run Arthur, Ari and Father Gregory down to the city to buy Arthur's new outfit. We'll use the cruiser. Siren if necessary."

"That's it, folks, everyone's got their marching orders. It's time to rock and roll," shouted Oscar, already running for the kitchen.

It was a mad dash to the door.

"Not quite," shouted Martin. They stopped. "Are you forgetting it's the end of summer?"

"What does that mean?" they yelled in chorus.

"Every flower bed in town is full of half-dead flowers."

"Karl," Mrs. Kruchinski yelled. "We need Karl," and she whipped out her mobile phone faster than a gunslinger.

"Still can't believe Mrs. K texts," said Berris.

And they were off....

CHAPTER 36
Frantic Preparations

Father Gregory and Ari ran straight to the barbershop. Walter had already finished Arthur's haircut and was giving him a shave.

"What's going on?" Arthur squirmed around in the chair.

"The wheels are in motion, and racing down the track faster than a runaway train," said Father Gregory. "I don't think I've ever felt the energy level in The Café as charged."

"Stop moving, Arthur. I've got a razor on your neck."

"Sorry, Walter. What could they possibly be doing?"

"The village is mobilized to make this the perfect evening for you and Ana Felicia. Everything from table settings to sprucing up the flower beds so she can see us at our best."

"My word," said Arthur. "So, what's next?"

"After this, it's over to Berris for a manicure and then into the city to buy a new suit, shirt, tie and shoes," said Ari.

"Do I really need a whole new outfit? I think my suit, with a good brushing...."

Ari interrupted.

"Arthur, you have a tidal wave barreling down on you. Best to start swimming as hard as you can."

Arthur's eyebrows shot straight up to his hairline. He managed a shaky nod.

A Romantic Table

Madge told Mrs. Kruchinski that Oscar wouldn't need her for a few hours and she'd be glad to help with the table setting.

"Thank you, Madge, I'll take all the help I can get."

The table was arranged. They stepped back to appraise their handiwork.

"What do you think?" asked Mrs. Kruchinski.

"It's stunning!" answered Madge. "It needs one last touch." She pulled out a strand of white twinkle lights from a bag and strung them around the fireplace.

"Enchanting," said Mrs. Kruchinski.

"The perfect setting for a marriage proposal, I should say."

"I wonder how much Ana Felicia has changed? They were kids when they last saw one another. Forty years ago? Although, if she looks like she does in the poster, she's still beautiful."

"Oh, that poster," said Mrs. Kruchinski with a grunt of disgust. "Those things are all airbrushed and did you notice it only showed her head? She could be 400 pounds under that neck."

"That's unkind," said Madge but couldn't resist a hearty laugh.

Madge's eyes widened as she looked at her watch. "I need to get going. You coming?"

"No, I'll wait for Constance to bring the flowers."

As soon as Madge left, Mrs. Kruchinski searched for the letter. She had to know what was in it. She was shocked to find two letters on Arthur's bed.

She read the recent letter first and thought, *Father Gregory was right. It just says she wants to ask him a question.*

Then she read the 40-year-old letter. *Arthur, you fool, how could you have left her? Marry her now...even if she is 400 pounds.*

Mrs. Kruchinski wanted to stay and wait for Constance but decided she'd better get back to the village and check on Karl's progress.

Constance Says Goodbye

After an hour of fussing with the flower arrangement, Constance stepped back. *It's perfect.* Suddenly, her eyes were stinging with tears. The arrangement was for Arthur's future bride.

Forgive me, Arthur. I'm truly happy for you and Ana Felicia. I can't seem to help myself, though. I wish it were me.

Constance went into the bathroom and patted cold water on her face. *Pull yourself together, old girl. Don't even think of ruining Arthur's night.*

Carefully placing the flowers in her shopping cart, she headed for Arthur's.

The dining table was exquisite. Twinkle lights playfully dancing off of the china, silver and crystal spoke of love and romance. And that candelabra! Stunning.

Constance placed her flowers in the middle of the table. *The finishing touch. A table fit for a queen.* Her eyes welled up again. *Hold it together, Constance.*

She looked around Arthur's home for the last time. Her old habit of fussing and tidying triggered without thought.

She straightened the papers on his desk and the stack of books and magazines on his coffee table. When she went to plump the pillows on the couch, she stopped.

"No more Friday night movies," she said aloud to the empty room.

A brutal loneliness took hold as she stood for the last time in the intimacy of Arthur's home. It was an unwelcome but familiar friend.

"Oh, Arthur, I miss you already," she cried out to no one.

That's enough! Constance fiercely shook her head so hard her neck bones creaked. Then, straightening her shoulders, she walked out the door.

"Goodbye, George. Take good care of him," she called out as she passed the beloved bench.

She met Birdie on her way back to the village.

"Everything ready?"

"Wait till you see the table, Birdie. It's dazzling."

And Birdie walked on, pretending she hadn't seen the redness in Constance's eyes.

Arthur Gets Ready

Arthur, Ari and Father Gregory arrived back home a little before 6 pm. The first thing they saw when they entered the house was the table setting.

"Ari, Gregory, look, isn't it beautiful?" Arthur said in wide-eyed wonder.

"It's a table set for a king and queen, Arthur," said Ari.

"Well, Ana Felicia is certainly a queen, but me a king is a stretch." And the three men shared a laugh and a high-five.

"I needed that," said Arthur. "This has been one tense day."

"Hang in there, my brother. The best is yet to come."

Arthur left to dress. He needed to decompress. He needed a large scotch. He needed to talk to George.

"I need a drink," said Ari. "Join me, Father?"

"I thought you'd never ask."

"Let's hope Arthur has a secret stash hidden around this joint."

Father Gregory looked heavenward in thanks as they saw the six bottles of wine on the kitchen counter.

Ari yelled out, "Arthur, you won't believe it, there's a truckload of wine out here." And as he examined the wine, he added, "Correction, there's a truckload of fine wine out here."

"Oh, that will be from Birdie."

"Birdie!" Father Gregory's mouth fell open.

"Yes, Birdie. She lived in Paris in her twenties and apparently developed a taste for fine wine."

"You're kidding, right?"

"No, it's true."

"What was she doing in Paris?"

"Studying art. She's a very fine artist. Even had her work in a bunch of Paris exhibitions. I've seen some. It's exceptional."

"How do you know all this?"

"I talk to people, Gregory."

"Well, I talk to people all the time and I don't seem to know as much as you do."

"No, you listen to people. And what people talk to priests about are their problems. Not their joys."

Father Gregory made a mental note. *Must turn that around.*

Arthur strolled into the kitchen.

"So, what do you think, gentlemen? Do I look as old as I feel?"

"Very dashing, old boy," said Father Gregory.

"Very dashing, indeed, Arthur." Ari handed his brother a glass of wine and then raised his glass. "To love and second chances."

"Here, here!"

They stepped onto the porch to swap stories and jokes to cover their nervousness and enjoy their wine in the coolness of the evening. When their glasses were empty, Father Gregory looked at his watch and announced, "It's showtime, gentlemen."

CHAPTER 37
The Visit

As the three men walked down the hill to the village, they met Oscar and Madge rolling a cart overflowing with food.

"Arthur, you look splendid," said Madge.

"Well done, Arthur," said Oscar. "We'll leave the food on warming plates and head back. Madge wants to see when Ana Felicia arrives."

"Can't thank you enough."

When they reached the village, the three men stopped dead. They couldn't believe how the old village gleamed.

Every shop window was newly washed and sparkling. The sidewalks were swept clean and the flowerbeds were all pruned, weeded and manicured. Stones End looked its absolute charming best.

"Mrs. Kruchinski has outdone herself," said Father Gregory.

"Outstanding, simply outstanding."

Then Arthur saw them. Villagers crammed in everywhere. They were in The Café, the bookshop, the bakery and even the barbershop. Dozens of folks pressed up against the windows and waving at him.

"Oh no," said Arthur. "What on Earth do they think they're doing?

Father Gregory saw sweat break out on Arthur's brow and went into action.

"Ari, you take this side of the street and I'll take the other. Keep everyone out of sight when Ana Felicia pulls up."

"Gotcha." Ari ran off.

"Now Arthur, calm down. This night is what you have been waiting 40 years for. Everything is going to be...."

"Gregory, her car! Hurry, hurry!"

Father Gregory dashed to The Café.

Arthur stood in the middle of Main Street watching Ana Felicia's limousine approach. His legs felt wobbly. "Hold on, Arthur," he said aloud.

His pulse raced and he felt the familiar heart-stopping breathlessness wash over him. *Don't faint now, old boy.*

The limousine stopped. The driver stepped out to open the rear door. Arthur held up his hand for him to wait. Arthur walked over, opened it himself and held out his hand to Ana Felicia.

"Nice touch," said Mrs. Kruchinski from The Café window. "I didn't think he had it in him."

"Get away from that window!" yelled Father Gregory.

Ana Felicia took Arthur's hand. "My dearest Arthur, how many years has it been?"

"It doesn't matter. Because right now, I'm 22 again and looking at the most beautiful woman in the world."

"And you look wonderful, Arthur. Just as I remembered you."

"Well, she's definitely not 400 pounds," said Madge who just rushed in, out of breath.

"No, she certainly is not," replied a drop-jawed Mrs. Kruchinski.

"Will you two get the away from that window!" yelled Oscar.

Ana Felicia took Arthur's arm and they walked up the hill to Stones End.

Their conversation felt familiar as though they were picking up from just yesterday.

Arthur pointed out two cranes flying overhead toward the river.

Ana Felicia laughed. "You still do that?"

"Do what?"

"Notice every movement of nature. You used to point out all sorts of things to me. Mother bird feeding a worm to her open-mouthed chicks. Gulls coming in for a landing on the water."

Arthur returned her laugh. "Yes, I guess I do."

"Thank you for not changing, Arthur. It's one of the things I loved most about you."

"I could say the same to you. You still laugh easily. It's my most cherished memory of you."

"I hope you have food waiting. We left Manhattan and didn't stop."

"We have a wonderful meal waiting for us. Roast lamb!"

"How did you know?"

"You like roast lamb?"

"It's my absolute favorite. Don't you remember?"

As they came upon the house, Ana Felicia saw the bench. She could see that it was made from love.

A three-masted schooner was carved in the middle of the wide back rail. To the right and left of the schooner were six fish and six cypress trees each representing a member of his family.

"Arthur, it's exquisite," she said as her hand lingered over the carvings. "It reminds me of home. Did you make it?"

"I did. Old George has been with me dozens of years."

"Old George? You gave it a name?" she said playfully.

"Yes, and George and I have had many rousing conversations."

She gave a musical laugh and Arthur thought, *I'm in heaven.*

Ana Felicia's face lit up when she saw the dining table. The flickering light from the candles made the crystal and china look ethereal and the flowers in the center of the table as though they were floating on air.

"It's perfect," she said clapping her hands together like an excited child. "Did you do all this yourself?"

"I'm tempted to say yes to impress you, but as it turns out, I have many wonderful friends."

"You're a lucky man, Arthur. Not everyone can say that. I certainly can't."

"How can that be true? You must have made hundreds of friends during your career."

"I had hundreds of people in my life but not many I could call a friend. But enough about me, I want to hear everything about your life. Don't you dare leave anything out. We have 40 years to catch up on."

"OK, but then it's your turn."

"Agreed."

Arthur had decided not to talk about the fateful night they parted. He said that he wanted their reunion to be about going forward.

So instead he told her about his new life in America. How his uncle left him the printing business and the house upon his passing. He talked about the village and everyone in it.

He told her about bossy, impossible Mrs. Kruchinski, who would try a saint's patience but underneath it all was pure mush and had a heart of gold.

"I like her," said Ana Felicia. "She seems to care deeply about this village and everyone in it."

"Sometimes a little too much," said Arthur and they shared a laugh.

He talked about Oscar and Madge.

"They have the perfect marriage, those two. Oscar is churlish and Madge is a saint. Their understanding and love of one another is real."

"That's beautiful, Arthur. They sound like soulmates."

"Yes. Two peas in a pod."

He described the village's Thursday night ritual of eating at The Café and how he and his best friend Constance never missed it. He went into great detail.

"Arthur, it sounds divine."

He talked about Constance and the tragedies she endured and how lucky he was to have found a fellow Scrabble player and movie buff.

"I like Constance, too," said Ana Felicia. "She's not only a survivor but came out from the other side of darkness with a joyful heart. Believe me, that's hard to do."

"Yes, I have the greatest respect for Constance. She's truly a grand lady."

Arthur delighted in telling Ana Felicia about their resident virtuoso Walter. "You've got to hear him. He has an exquisite tenor voice and loves opera."

"Really? How wonderful. And right here in Stones End."

"Right here at the barbershop. Yes, we are very fortunate. Walter gives a mini-concert the first Friday of each month."

"I would love to hear him. Where is it held?"

"Don't laugh, he sings in front of his barbershop."

"That sounds marvelous, Arthur, and great fun."

He talked about Martin and how he thinks he's a character straight out of a Charles Dickens novel. Ana Felicia enjoyed hearing about Martin.

"I hope he gets his dream and makes it to England."

"And Berris, what can I say about Berris? Stuck in the 1960s. She fears change on a monumental level, lots of psychedelic everything and very colorful hair. But at the end of the day, Berris is a kind, uncomplicated soul."

"If I ever get to meet her, I have to remember to ask her about that spray-in hair color."

Arthur shook his head and laughed.

"And then there's Birdie. She's probably the most complex character in Stones End and I haven't quite figured her out yet."

Arthur spoke of all her wonderful antics and Ana Felicia agreed, "Complex, absolutely."

"Is she as crazy as everyone thinks?"

"No, not in the least."

"Interesting, very interesting," she replied.

"I almost forgot Caroline. She's the deputy sheriff and has a brilliant mind. Reads too many murder mysteries and sees evil where none exists. But she's a good soul and will lend a helping hand to anyone who needs it, even stray animals."

"Arthur Covington, you are one lucky man. To live in a village like this with all these wonderful, amazing people who care about you and care for you."

"Yes. My life is blessed."

"You are the richest man I know and I mean that sincerely. Hang onto this, Arthur. It's priceless. Worth fighting for, that's for sure."

"I guess I am." His brows drew together.

"OK, young lady, it's your turn."

"Yes, but I have to stretch. I'm getting stiff."

"Oh, I know that feeling."

They poured themselves another glass of wine and went out to the porch.

I could get used to this, Ana Felicia thought. *Living here. Having real friends. Please, Arthur, say yes.*

CHAPTER 38
The Long Wait

"I can't stand this waiting!" exclaimed Mrs. Kruchinski. "I wonder how it's going between those two lovebirds."

Madge agreed. "I know. I'd give anything to have my ear pressed up against the window of Arthur's dining room right about now."

"Calm down, you two. We'll know soon enough," said Oscar.

Mrs. Kruchinski leaned close to Madge and whispered, "Where's Martin?"

"Next door at The Page Turner. Why?"

"Do you think we should send him up to Arthur's? You know, without being seen."

"Wish I had thought of that. He'll go if we ask. I'll run next door."

But as Madge got up, she felt a hand on her shoulder pushing her back into her seat.

"You two have clearly lost your minds," said Father Gregory. "Don't even think of such a despicable thing."

Mrs. Kruchinski and Madge hung their heads. Father Gregory knew they were only sorry they got caught.

Walter called out: "Father, stop being a stick in the mud. Let Martin go take a peek. The suspense is killing us."

Birdie backed Walter. "That's right, Padre, we can be planning the wedding as we wait. But if Ana Felicia is up there yelling Arthur's head off, we need to know, so we don't waste our time."

The wagons are circling, thought Father Gregory. He looked in Caroline's direction for help.

"You're on your own, Father. I'll jump in if they get unruly."

"Thanks for that."

Oscar finally put a stop to it all. "Everyone just settle down. No more talk about spying on Arthur and Ana Felicia. Don't make me throw you all out."

Father Gregory shot Oscar a grateful look and wondered how Ari was faring at The Page Turner. *Hope he's not under siege.*

CHAPTER 39
Ana Felicia's Story

A cool breeze stirred and Arthur went into the house to fetch a throw.

Ana Felicia sat in the peace of the bucolic scene before her. She was already feeling like Stones End was home.

She was desperately counting on Arthur wanting her in his life again. *What if he doesn't feel the same?* she thought. *Do I even have the right to barge in on his wonderful world?*

The full moon cast dappled shadows over the riverbank and made the water sparkle with tiny moonlight diamonds.

The odd chirp of a cricket hanging on to the last vestiges of summer could be heard far off in the distance. Late summer roses scented the night air and Ana Felicia was sure she could see frogs hopping along the riverbank in some kind of a lunar dance.

Oh, I could be very happy here.

Arthur returned and Ana Felicia said in a dreamy voice, "This is divine."

"Yes, it's my favorite time of night to sit out here with George."

"And what do you and George talk about?"

"Sorry, George and I have a hard and fast rule. What's said on the bench, stays on the bench."

And Ana Felicia let out another musical laugh. Arthur thought again, *I'm in heaven.*

"You're stalling," he said playfully. "I'm waiting to hear all the thrilling details of your life and worldwide travels."

"Arthur, it was anything but thrilling."

"Did you lose your love for singing?"

"No, no. Singing is still my passion and always will be. I'm lucky I have that. It got me through all the bad times."

Ana Felicia took Arthur's lead. She avoided what happened the night of her debut. She started with what happened afterward.

"I married Sebastian Atros whom my father chose for me. He came from a wealthy, old island family and gave me and the children everything."

"It makes me happy to hear that."

"Well, hold that thought. The price for a life of luxury and social prominence was for me to turn a blind eye to all his failings."

"What are you saying?"

"That he had an eye for other women."

"I'm so sorry, Ana Felicia. I would never have imagined."

"At first, he was very attentive. I couldn't say I loved him. But I respected that he was my husband and the father of our children. It wasn't long before he had one affair after another."

"The thought of you spending your life unhappy is crushing

to me."

"He was always discreet, and I was thankful for that. But when I first learned of his philandering, I was furious at the thought of putting up with it for the rest of my life."

"I can only imagine, my dear."

"But then I thought of my children and how I didn't want them to be part of a broken family. They loved their father very much and never knew what was really going on."

"That was a noble decision."

"And, sadly, one that many people are forced to make."

"Yes. A harsh reality for some."

"But my children are the love of my life. They're bright, fun and funny. I brought them up to be decent and respectful. I'm so very proud of them."

"I love thinking of you as a mother. Was your husband a good father?"

"No. He didn't have much interest in the kids. He'd float in every month or so buying their love with an armload of presents."

"Sounds like you raised your kids alone. And you had the role of disciplinarian and he was the good guy."

"Good guy. An oxymoron if I ever heard one. The truth is, he was a horrid man."

"Didn't want to be that direct. But, yes, he certainly sounded like one."

Talk of Sebastian darkened the mood. Ana Felicia's eyes went hard. Her mouth twisted in anger or was it pain? Arthur knew he had to change the subject...and fast.

"Tell me about your kids."

Her eyes softened immediately.

"Monica is married with a family of her own and that makes me a grandmother. Can you imagine? They fill my heart and soul with love, joy and purpose."

"A grandmother. Surely, you're too young."

"You always were a charmer, Arthur Covington."

"Helena is seven and Oliver five. We spend Christmas, Easter and whatever time I can steal them away during summertime. It's never enough."

"How about your other kids?"

"Only one more. My son, Matthew. He's a production manager at La Scala in Milan. He's married to his job. I worry about the long hours he works, but I suppose that's what mothers do."

"My mother certainly was a worrier when it came to her kids."

"A year ago, my husband died. It was one of those bittersweet moments. Bitter in that we never really had a life together and sweet in that I was finally free."

"You certainly earned your freedom, my dear."

"At first, there was guilt at how liberated I felt but I let those feelings go. I was free to live as I please. Does that sound selfish?"

"No, my dearest, it doesn't."

"I had no ill feelings for him as I stood at his grave. All feelings for him left me years before. So, I prayed for his soul and closed that chapter of my life."

"Never easy saying goodbye, no matter the circumstances."

"So here I am, Arthur, getting ready to end my career. And it made me think of you since you were there at the start."

"Gracious of you to say. We both know I wasn't."

"You were, dearest. I was ready to run. You were the one who got me through my debut which catapulted my career."

"I never thought of it like that."

"I was scared to walk on the stage as a young girl. Now as an old woman, I'm scared to walk off."

"I understand. I won't let myself think about retiring."

"I can't face it alone, Arthur. Which brings me to the question I came to ask."

Ana Felicia suddenly stood. She was biting her lip and slowly pacing.

"What it is, my dear?"

"I'm a little nervous to ask you this."

"No, no, don't be. You can ask me anything."

So, Ana Felicia asked and Arthur, of course, said yes.

"Arthur, you've made me so happy. I simply can't find the

words. Not to have to face the future alone."

She clasped her hands together tightly as though trying to hold onto the moment. Her eyes sparkled with joy.

"And I promise to stay put this time." Arthur gave her a bear hug.

"I can't wait for you to meet my family. You will fall in love with them and they with you."

Arthur was beaming at seeing Ana Felicia so happy and knowing he was the source made it all the more satisfying.

"I'm overjoyed, my dear. I'd given up hope many years ago of ever seeing you again. And now this astonishing turn of events."

Ana Felicia's mood suddenly turned pensive.

"I know we agreed that we wouldn't talk about our past."

Arthur stiffened like he'd stepped on a shorted wire.

"There's a question that has been tormenting me for 40 years. Why did you leave without saying goodbye?"

Arthur wanted to escape. Anywhere.

"I created my own version of why you left. One that I understood. I didn't like it, but I did understand. Doubt crept in each night, though."

A pain shot through Arthur like an old war wound.

"There was a letter explaining everything. I wish I could say why I never mailed it, but I didn't."

"What did it say?"

"It said how proud I was of you. That you sang like an angel."

"I love hearing that."

"I met your father in the garden that night. He was with your future husband."

Ana Felicia nodded.

"Your father demanded that I stop seeing you. That your hand was already promised."

"Oh, Arthur." She could see the pain in his eyes.

"It was clear your father would fight to come between us. That would tear your family apart, Ana Felicia. I didn't want that for you or for us."

Ana Felicia held her hand to her heart sharing his sadness.

"I thought your husband was someone who could give you all the things I couldn't. Give you the life you deserved."

"That's a fairy tale."

"Of course. I didn't know at the time how your husband would mistreat you."

"Can I share an ironic twist to our story? One that will shock you, I think. It certainly shocked me."

"Absolutely."

"On my father's deathbed, he told me about your meeting in the garden. He told me how he threatened you and the awful things Sebastian said to you."

A dark cloud passed over Arthur's face as he remembered his humiliation.

"Then my father spoke your parting words. 'My name is Arthur Covington,' you said. 'I wanted you to know the name of the man who loves your daughter more than life itself.'"

"I remember that. I was angry at your father's arrogance and just blurted it out."

"He related to me that your statement was a simple one, but powerful. It made him doubt himself."

"How?"

"You made him wonder if you were the better choice for my happiness."

"Well, you have shocked me. I didn't think your father was capable of such feelings."

"Yes, it surprised me too. We both know, however, he brushed these feelings aside to justify his own plans for my life."

"Yes. He was a manipulator. Pulling everyone's strings."

"But here's the real shocker. Before his last breath, he whispered, 'I'm sorry, my child.'"

"Well, I'll be damned."

"Apologizing. Another first for my father. A tragic ending. Don't you think?"

Arthur turned his head and glared at the river beyond. He

dared not look at Ana Felicia fearing his emotions would betray him.

The old wretch knew! He felt an age-old rage for what Ana Felicia's father stole from them.

But for the first time in 40 long years, he knew with certainty that his decision to leave was right. Her father would never relent. Death was the only thing that softened the hardness of his miserable heart.

"Arthur, are you alright?"

"Yes, my dear, I'm fine," he said patting her hand. "And I agree. A tragic ending. He squandered his life to satisfy his own needs and, in the end, missed out on a relationship with his only child. Very sad."

"Yes. It is for me."

The story drained them. They both stared blankly into the night. Then Ana Felicia gave a long stretch. "Come, my dear, it's time to walk me home. Or, at least, to my limo."

Arthur squeezed her hand. "Your chariot awaits, m'lady."

As they walked back to the village, they held hands as young lovers do.

"I hope you can attend my final performance."

"Try and stop me."

Arthur opened the door to the limousine. Before Ana Felicia entered, they embraced.

"This is a familiar feeling," Arthur whispered.

"You always make me feel safe and loved, Arthur." They kissed briefly and then she was gone.

Arthur stood in the middle of the street watching as Ana Felicia's limousine drove away. Thoughts of the wonderful evening were still playing in his mind when Father Gregory and Ari rushed toward him.

Father Gregory reached Arthur first. "Well, did she ask the question?"

"Yes, she did."

"And?" said Ari bursting.

"I said yes."

And with that, Father Gregory turned to the waiting neighbors, threw both arms high in the air and yelled, "He said yes!"

A roar of cheers erupted that should have blown the roof clear off every shop in Stones End.

Out of the corner of his eye, Father Gregory noticed the curtain on Constance's window fall back into place. The priest looked quickly at Arthur. He saw it too.

"You should talk to her, Arthur. I hear today was hard for Constance. After all, her world as it relates to you is about to change drastically."

"Yes, it is," said Arthur.

"Best to get it over with," said Ari.

CHAPTER 40
The End of a Crazy
Mixed-up Day

A rthur took a long breath before knocking.

Constance opened the door with a happy face but he saw her eyes were red.

"Come in, come in. I'm dying to hear how the evening went. Do you want a drink?"

"No, thanks, Constance. Is it too late for a chat? There's something I have to talk to you about."

"Of course not. I'm all ears."

Constance didn't know who looked worse. She with her puffy eyes or Arthur who was pacing and wringing his hands.

"Sure you don't want a drink?"

"On second thought, I'll take one."

"Absolutely, white or red?"

"Got any scotch?"

"You're making me nervous. Scotch conversations are always more serious than wine conversations," she said. A laugh caught in her throat.

She handed Arthur his drink then braced herself for the unwelcome news. She felt like a prisoner waiting to be sentenced.

"Constance, this has been a crazy, mixed-up day and one full of surprises."

He took a gulp of scotch for courage.

Arthur related the details of his reunion with Ana Felicia. How they reminisced about Greece and shared all that had happened these past 40 years.

Constance was genuinely happy for Arthur's good fortune yet listened with a heavy heart. She knew how this story would end.

"I heard Father Gregory. You said yes. I'm so happy for you and Ana Felicia."

"That's what I need to talk to you about, Constance."

She reached across the couch and touched his hand. "Please, Arthur, you don't owe me an explanation."

"I do, Constance. You're my best friend and there's something I want you to know. Can I share a journey I've been on today? It may help explain things."

"Of course." It was the last time she would have Arthur to herself. She was in no hurry.

Arthur took another gulp of scotch.

"Ana Felicia and I had a doomed love affair when we were kids. Her father was against us. He was a powerful man who threatened me and my family if I didn't stop seeing her."

"What did you do?"

Arthur was staring past Constance as though she wasn't there. She could see the answer caused pain.

"I left her," he said. "He would have made our lives miserable. I knew in my heart we didn't stand a chance."

"And you never saw Ana Felicia again until tonight?"

"Never. But for the past 40 years, I've been tormented by it. Why didn't I fight for the woman I loved?"

"Isn't the answer that you two didn't stand a chance?"

"Yes and no. Which brings me to today's journey."

"Go on."

"The day started with the feeling that I had come to the end of a jigsaw puzzle only to find pieces missing."

"That's frustrating."

"George was convinced that Ana Felicia's letter held the missing pieces. Gregory too. But I knew the answer didn't lie there."

"Why not?"

"I couldn't say why at the start of the day. But I knew with certainty that nothing in Ana Felicia's letter would give me the answer."

"Well, if the answer wasn't coming from Ana Felicia, then it had to come from you."

"Exactly. You see, I lived the past four decades in the shadow of our love affair. The memory was precious to me. And I fought against losing it."

"And you thought opening the letter threatened your memory somehow?"

"I did. Best to leave things be. That's how I felt. But throughout today, small clues led me to think differently."

"Were you ready to leave the past behind?" Constance offered.

"Yes. George and Gregory agreed. They were pushing me toward a future that held the hope of love."

A knot twisted in her stomach.

"I found the first piece of the puzzle as I reminisced about my parents. It didn't hit home right away but the memory caused a bell to strike."

"Not following you yet. But go on." She wasn't seeing where this was going. But the end of the story meant Arthur would leave. She hung onto the moments.

"The second piece of the puzzle came from something Ana Felicia said. She told me how lucky I was to live among such wonderful people. It was worth fighting for. The bell struck again."

"We are blessed to live here, Arthur." She couldn't bring herself to say aloud what she was really thinking. *You found a reason to fight for Ana Felicia's love.*

"It was then the last piece to the puzzle appeared. And the final bell chimed."

Arthur finished his scotch in one long gulp. He sat deadly still not knowing how to continue. *How can I say this to her? Should I just blurt it out? No, you'll sound like a fool. Think, Arthur. Think.*

Constance moved to the edge of her seat. *Oh God, this is it.* She wrapped her arms around her waist waiting for the blow to land.

Arthur's face twisted in torment. She knew he didn't want to hurt her.

Constance couldn't bear seeing him in such agony on her account. *Just put an end to this misery.*

She looked at the kind, humble man struggling to let her down gently. It moved her to ask the question that would separate them forever.

"What was the final piece to the puzzle?"

Arthur's stare was fixed. "Not what, Constance. Who...."

He took hold of her hands, gave an apologetic shrug and said, "Can you forgive a foolish old man for having no eyes to see with and no ears to hear with all these years?"

"My God," her hand covered her heart. "It's Alastair Sim's line from 'A Christmas Carol.'"

"Constance Whitestead, you're the final piece to the puzzle. You are the bell that rang out with perfect clarity."

Then Arthur went down on one knee. "My journey ends at your doorstep, Constance. I'm in love with you and our beautiful life. Would you do me the honor of marrying me?"

Constance sat very still staring into her lap. This was so sudden. She didn't see it coming. Questions collided in her head.

Arthur couldn't tell if she was in shock or didn't want to marry him and was thinking of a polite way to decline.

"What is it, Constance?"

"Arthur, forgive me, but I have to ask. Did Ana Felicia propose marriage to you?"

"No, Constance, she didn't."

"Oh," said Constance. She tried to hold her mouth from falling open but couldn't relax her furrowed brow.

"Well, then I have to know. If she had asked you to marry her, what would your answer have been?"

"My answer would have been no. You see, Constance, I finally knew why I didn't fight for Ana Felicia."

"Why?"

"The life Ana Felicia and I would have wasn't strong enough to fight for. That hit me like a ton of bricks. I loved her my whole life. I love her still. But I realized that I'm not in love with her."

"No?"

"No. For me, it's not enough to just love a person. I must love the life I have with them. There's a harmony to having both. It's what my parents had. It's what I've always wanted."

"I think I see."

"Think of it. Can you truly love a person when you hate the

life you have with them? You'd never have harmony."

"I do understand. But I'll beg another question. Did you consider asking Ana Felicia to marry you?"

"No, Constance. I'd have to give up my life with you to do that."

Constance felt her joy starting to push back her doubts but she needed to ask one final question.

"Arthur, dearest, are you sure?" She held her breath.

"Constance Whitestead, I would stand at the gates of hell and fight Satan himself before I ever let you go out of my life."

That was all Constance needed to hear. Her fears vanished. Her tears flowed. "I can't find the words to describe my happiness."

"Now, I'm getting a little stiff down here. So, let me repeat. I love you, Constance. Your love is the reason I exist. Will you marry me?"

Wiping her tears, Constance said, "I love you, Arthur, you dear man. Yes, I will marry you."

Arthur reached into his pocket and produced a ring box.

"It was my grandmother's ring," Arthur said with tenderness. "And the box, Constance, the box was made in the Greek village where I grew up. And it's the color of the water my father and I looked upon every day."

And then Arthur opened the box.

"It's perfect. Simply perfect."

He placed the ring on Constance's finger.

"Help me up. I want to kiss my future bride."

And Arthur sensed that all-too-familiar feeling of his heart stopping. Only this time, he felt an ache in his stomach as well. *I went with my gut on this one, Pop.*

"I couldn't sleep if I tried. You wanna watch a movie?" he said. He wrapped his arms around Constance. She melted into him.

"No, my darling. I'm going to The Café and announce our engagement. Want to come?"

He flashed his broadest smile. "Wouldn't miss it for the world, my dear. I want to see the look on Olga's face."

Arthur and Constance walked into The Café. Constance raised her left hand, wiggled her ring finger and shouted, "We're engaged!"

The room looked as though someone shot a stun gun. Mrs. Kruchinski hit the floor in a dead faint.

Madge was the first to recover and ran to Constance.

"I hoped and hoped for years and then gave up hope. And now here you are with a ring on your finger. I'm so happy for you, I don't know what to do."

Walter pumped Arthur's hand. "Couldn't be happier for you both, Arthur. You old son of a gun."

"Champagne on the house!" Oscar yelled.

Arthur weaved through the crowd of well-wishers to where

Ari and Father Gregory stood grinning like two Cheshire cats.

"You're pretty good at the old bait-and-switch, brother."

"You should play poker, Arthur. You have the best poker face I've ever seen."

"I'm sorry about that, Gregory. I thought Constance should be the first to know."

"Perfectly understandable, my friend. But I'll expect you in confession all the same for your lie about Ana Felicia asking the question," he laughed.

"That part is true. Ana Felicia did ask me a question and I did say yes."

Just then, Karl revived Mrs. Kruchinski who sat up and loudly announced, "We have a wedding to plan! Karl, get me off this dirty floor."

Mrs. Kruchinski hugged Arthur. "I'm so thrilled, Arthur. You finally came to your senses. A little late but better late than never."

"Constance, will you be wearing a day dress or a gown?" she shouted over the noise in the packed room.

"Can't keep a good woman down," Karl laughed.

"What an extraordinary day," said Arthur. "But I have to say, I'm happy to see it end."

"Well, get a good night's sleep, brother of mine. Because tomorrow you start planning the wedding. And trust me, you'll think today was kiddie play compared to that."

Arthur and Father Gregory shot one another a look of sheer panic.

🌣·🌣

And Birdie thought, *who shall I be for the wedding? Someone grand I should think.*

And Caroline thought, *thank God, Arthur didn't murder Ana Felicia.*

And Berris thought, *Constance should have pink hair for the wedding.*

And Walter smiled and sang, "Con te partiro."

And Martin wondered, *what could Ana Felicia have asked Arthur?*

CHAPTER 41
One Final Task

Arthur poured himself a glass of wine and headed out to the porch.

"Quite a day, George."

"One of your finest, Arthur."

"Yes. None better. By the way, were you shocked Constance and I ended up together?"

"No. I've known for 30 years that you two would tie the knot."

"Well then, I'm the one who's shocked that you never said anything."

"I knew you'd get there eventually. So, tell me, Arthur, how does it feel? Out of the shadows and facing the sun?"

"Pretty damn good, George."

Arthur looked at the river as though he were seeing it for the first time. The moonlight appeared as brilliant lights shooting off its surface. Moonbeam fireworks just for him.

Yes, good, indeed, he thought.

He finished the mouthful of wine.

"One last thing, George."

"What's that?"

"Thank you. I couldn't have done it without you."

"My pleasure, Arthur."

Arthur walked toward the front door.

"I'm glad you finally took my advice and went with your gut."

Arthur smiled. "I thought that might be you. Goodnight, Pop."

"Pleasant dreams, son."

Hello Fellow Reader:

Please accept my warm thanks for taking the time to read Turning Toward the Sun. I'm hoping that you enjoyed getting to know Arthur and the wonderful and lively residents of Stones End.

I'm happy to say, the second book in the series is in the works. Untitled to date, but a sneak peek of Chapter 1 is waiting for you on my website at www.ceilwarren.com.

And it would make Mrs. Kruchinski's day if you had a moment to post a review of Turning Toward the Sun. Just visit my website and she'll tell you how in her know-it-all fashion.

Feel free to contact me anytime: contact@ceilwarren.com. You can also find me on Facebook, Twitter and LinkedIn.

All the best and happy reading,

Ceil Warren

How to use this book in your book club discussion group.

We never get to hear what Ana Felicia asked Arthur. We know she didn't propose marriage. So, what could her question possibly have been?

It appears that Ana Felicia and Arthur will continue their relationship as friends. Can you ever think of your first love as just a friend?

Will Constance have a problem with the friendship between Ana Felicia and Arthur?

Should Constance be worried that the love between Ana Felicia and Arthur will resurface?

George tells Arthur that a person's lowest moment doesn't define who you are. Do you agree?

Why doesn't Ana Felicia share a lot of details about her husband with Arthur?

What was the final piece of the puzzle for Arthur?

Does Martin have it in him to leave Stones End and move to England?

Arthur tells George that one night long ago he and Birdie shared bits of their tragic stories with one another. What tragedy could Birdie have faced in her past?

Have you ever been faced with a troubling issue where your friends came to your aid?

About the Author – Ceil Warren

Native New Yorker Ceil Warren builds on a long family line of storytellers and characters faced with life's impossible challenges. Born into a close-knit family of eight children, she grew up with amazing tales and people from Newfoundland to Belarus. Stories of survival: from Manhattan tenements in the 1920s to an exploding ship in World War II.

Living 17 miles north of Manhattan in Westchester County, Ceil takes full advantage of Broadway theater, museums, ballet and opera. All nourish her creative passion for storytelling, characters and drama.

Ceil shattered the glass ceiling for business women and corporate leaders in the 1970s, when women were just beginning to advance into higher-level management and corporate positions. She self-taught her way to a successful career in finance, becoming CFO of a sales operation for a Fortune 500 company at the age of 34.

In her second career in writing, Ceil gladly trades building business plans, telling company stories and crunching numbers for weaving remarkable tales about people against all odds and places you want to visit or even make your home.

The reader will begin their journey into this first-in-a-series book, Turning Toward the Sun, in the imaginary village of Stones End, Connecticut. The story reveals the secrets, fears, passions and challenges of many of the quirky residents and provides a witty, poignant and delicious escape from the real world.

Made in the USA
Columbia, SC
04 January 2021

30248825R00138